Karma Rose
presents...

Cinderella
Dances

Cinderella Dances,
First Edition

by Karma Rose

ISBN: 978-1-7344914-3-2

First paperback edition, published 2020

Cover image model: Emily Miller.

This book is a work of fiction. Names, characters, places, and incidents are products of the author's imagination or are used fictitiously.

For my husband.
Thank you for believing in my aspirations
and supporting my ambition.

Love you more.

Accidents Happen

None of this was supposed to happen.

The thought possessed me, body and soul, as I took in the face of the woman lying there. The first thing I could feel was glad—glad that she wasn't awake to recognize me. Not because I knew her so well or some other drama. My reason was far more mundane because, truthfully, I knew so little of this woman. What disquieted me was how well she knew me—five minutes a day, five days a week, for the last three months, and she knew more of my habits than most of my coworkers.

She worked at the chicken place nearest my hospital. I stopped by for lunch each day, and she always took my order. It was a fact of life I had acknowledged nearly two months ago when she had my order cooking before I walked in and bagged by the time I reached the front of the line.

I should have known something was wrong when she wasn't there today, but I hadn't thought about it. I didn't even know her name, yet now I was staring her bruised, damaged body in the face with nothing to say, no way to compensate.

"Doctor? Doctor!" My assistant caught my attention abruptly, startling me back to reality. "We need to operate immediately."

I nodded once, determination settling in where my guilt had taken residence. "Of course. Ready the operating room."

~~ * ~ * ~ * ~~

"How's your cat?"
"I'm sorry?"

1

Karma Rose

The woman smiled. "Your cat. You said that she had an infection and you were worried about her, last week. How is she?"

I had stopped where I was, shocked by the fact that she had remembered when I couldn't even recall telling her. But that was just a memory now, a ghost of the girl who could stand. Now, I had to look all of that kindness in the eye and deliver the bad news.

When she saw me walk into the room she smiled, a strangely heart-wrenching sight after her accident. "Doctor. I never thought I'd be seeing you here."

I attempted to return the smile, no matter how strained it may be. "Well, you weren't at the restaurant, Miss Crowley, so I decided to come here for lunch."

She laughed quietly at me, and I could see how worried she was becoming. "So, Doctor Li. What happened? Why am I here?"

This I could do, this I could say. I had delivered very similar news countless times before. "You were in an accident, walking to work. Your head hit the pavement rather hard, so it's expected if you have difficulty with your recollection of the event."

She nodded slowly, a look of dread contorting her expression. "Okay. What else? Why can't I feel my legs? Doctor Li? Doctor?"

There it was again, that guilt. *She shouldn't be here.* "Where the car hit you—There's damage to your lower spine. We operated immediately, to do what we could, but...We won't know anything for certain for several weeks, at least."

"You mean I might never walk again?" she choked on her words, the sound wrenching the heart in my chest. I'd given the same news dozens of times before. This time shouldn't have been any different.

But my eyes refused to meet hers as I nodded. "It is a possibility, but there is a chance that, with treatment and physical therapy, in a couple of years..."

"In a couple of years, I won't have a job. Or a home," she replied faintly, trying so hard to be brave, I could see it. Every day for the last three months, she had helped me without even a sincere thanks to take home. Now, when there was the opportunity to return

2

her efforts, I didn't know how; I'd never cared enough to learn.

"I'm sorry," was all I could think to reply with, loathing how the seconds dragged by in agonizing silence. "If you need anything, please don't hesitate to call the nurse. She'll help to make you as comfortable as possible."

With that, I turned to leave, at once grateful and regretful that there was nothing left to say. No way to help and no way to lie anymore about the severity of her condition. Nothing to do but move on.

"Wait!" Her outcry stopped me short, and I was glad for it, though I didn't look back at her. "Thank you."

I winced at the words, but I was far from any mood to interpret my reactions at this point. I nodded curtly. "You're welcome."

~~ * ~ * ~ * ~~

Three days.

That was all, but I still couldn't seem to get away from that woman, Elaine. Months after first meeting her, I finally knew her name and now I couldn't get it out of my head.

"Hey, Li, you all right? Your head doesn't seem to be in the game today." Mark brought my attention back to the game of chess we were engaged in like we did every Saturday morning. Doctor Hart was a colleague of mine. Having met in college, we'd remained close friends since.

I took in the game and, with a quiet sigh, brought my knight to check. "What do you mean? I'm going to win."

He made a narrow escape by sacrificing a bishop, nodding. "But you usually beat me a lot sooner. If I didn't know better, I'd say I almost had a fighting chance."

That made me smile. "But you still know better, Mark."

"Okay. How about a bargain? I win, you tell me what's bothering you," he continued persistently.

"And what if I win?" I captured the sacrificial bishop, one

move closer to victory.

"I'll spring for dinner," was his immediate reply, moving forward a pawn rather than defending his king.

"I'm agreeable." My knight moved forward. "Check."

His queen struck from nowhere, throwing me off guard. Mark grinned. "Checkmate."

I stared at the setup, taking it in slowly, praying there was a way out. "Of all the times for you to improve..."

"So." He leaned back with a triumphant smile. "Who is she?"

"What?" I stared at him in shock. "That is a rather bold assumption."

"Well, it was that or drugs," he replied offhandedly. "So, again, who is she?"

I sighed quietly in defeat, shaking my head slowly. "I should have known you never would have bought me dinner."

He smiled patiently. "I'm waiting, Li."

"I never agreed to a time frame."

"No, but you still agreed," he pointed out with a smug smirk.

I nodded slowly, weighing my options. After all, guilt aside, there was no need to be unnerved by anything to do with Elaine. She was simply another unfortunate patient that I happened to recognize. Nothing more.

"All right. One of my patients—"

"Oh, *really*?!"

"—I just recognize her, that's all," I finished firmly, not wanting him to get the wrong idea. "Honestly, I may just be tired, she may have nothing at all to do with this. We *have* been busy," I added for extra effect. My efforts were met with a disbelieving scowl.

"You've gone seventy-two hours without sleep and still never lost to me before," he countered earnestly. "I'd like to know: Is she pretty? I mean, what kind of girl catches the eye of the great and stoic Doctor Li?"

I shot him a glare. "One who isn't my patient, Mark."

"So, we only have a few weeks to find out, then, huh?" He shrugged. "I can wait."

"Please, Mark, spare me. You're coming dangerously close to sounding perverted," I threatened him. Much to my dismay, it seemed to have very little effect on him.

"Takes one to know one, but you're getting away from the topic of interest." He stared me in the eye and asked, "Who is she?"

<u>Learning Elaine</u>

What an excellent question, Mark.

Who *is* Elaine Crowley?

At first, I assumed she was no one. But as the question burrowed deeper into my skin, I began to wonder. Who was the woman I was treating? Who was the woman I was coming to miss in my daily routine, as three days turned into three weeks?

I tried to occupy myself, to keep myself from being driven mad by this coincidence. But, after each time I treated her, I found that I wanted to know. I needed to know who everyone was that visited her, why each person reacted as though she had died when she herself gave them the news.

Who was Elaine?

The times I had seen her, she was an extraordinary employee at a second-rate store, nothing more than one of my habits. As I observed and listened, I learned that she was the oldest of three sisters, although her family rarely visited her. When they did, she almost seemed worse for it.

Her friends were there nearly every minute of every day during visiting hours, twenty or more people, each taking turns with the vigil as they kept her company. All of this made me want to know more, to understand. With much thanks to the Internet, I discovered that she was a dancer, and every one of her videos became more spirited and moving than the last as she grew older and her style matured. She had been utterly breathtaking.

To think that her entire life ended with what I had to say was far from unjust. It was cruel.

"Doctor Li! My man, how's it been?" greeted one of her more eccentric friends, Harry.

"I've been fine, thank you," I replied numbly, unable to look away from the woman in the bed. She had two of her friends adoring her, one painting her fingers, the other her toes. When I saw the absolute joy on Elaine's face, all I could think of was watching her dance. My heart seemed to stop in my chest.

Elaine looked up, turning all of that unrelenting happiness on me. "Oh, hello, Doctor Li. How are you?"

"I—" My throat closed, refusing to allow me to lie to her. "Not so well. I actually have some...unfortunate news."

"If it's about the insurance, we can take care of it," interjected the girl painting her fingers, Carol. "Right, Harry?"

"Anything for Elaine," he agreed.

"No, the insurance isn't the problem," I corrected quietly, but everyone had fallen silent, making it feel like I was screaming my next words. "The treatment didn't work. I'm so sorry, Elaine," I told her, sincerely wishing there was something more I could do.

She stared at me silently as my words slowly crushed all of the hope I could see fading from her eyes. "No. Please."

Her friends couldn't speak, barely able to move while Elaine herself simply nodded. Where her hope had been I saw strength as she pulled herself together, comforting the girls crying at her bedside.

"I'm sorry," I said again, realizing I truly had brought the news that Elaine Crowley was dead.

Her ghost looked me in the eye with a sad smile. "Thank you."

"Geez. Wow, that sucks," was all the support that Mark had to spare.

"Your comfort is overwhelming," I replied dryly, unable to do anything aside from staring at the pristine chessboard. Nearly twenty minutes, I still hadn't made a move.

"I know of a few very comforting liquors," he offered rhetorically. "Really, I don't see why you're so..."

"Upset?"

"Depressed," he corrected me, but I couldn't seem to care more than a grunt. "Exactly. First, there is no girl. You said so yourself. If you're not attached, then why are you caring about this one patient when you've never given a crap before?"

I frowned thoughtfully, staring at my queen. "Because I do care. Mark, if you'd seen...It's like I was the coroner, declaring her dead."

He nodded slowly. "There are other treatments, you know."

"None that her insurance would cover," I replied bitterly, finding myself upset over this universal injustice.

"No, but you could," he corrected me. I had to take a moment to understand what he was saying. If I took her treatment into my own hands...

"But I couldn't do that until the case is closed, anyway. And if it didn't work again..." I stopped myself from completing that sentence. "I don't think I should try anymore. She has a better chance —"

"With some other doctor once she leaves your care?" interrupted Mark heatedly. "You honestly think she'd walk again from them if *you* couldn't help her?"

"No, but I don't want to chance making things any worse for her than they already are," I explained, although it felt more like a fight to justify why I was backing down. Far from the truth, but good enough to swallow.

"Stop it, Li," he snapped. "From what you've been telling me about her, she's already hit rock bottom. Either help her out or stop whining, 'cause everyone else already knows that you're lying to yourself."

"How can I help someone I don't even know?" I asked. I was glad he could see sense when I was blinded by this problem.

He shrugged. "Then get to know her."

<u>Standing Still</u>

A week later, she was sent home.

For some reason, that saddened me—knowing that I would no longer see Elaine surrounded by loving friends who, I had the feeling, would kill for her if it would make her better. Unfortunately, it wouldn't, or I may have considered helping them.

"Doctor, are you all right?"

I shook my head slowly. "No, I don't feel well. I may put in a half-day and go home after lunch."

My assistant nodded. "Understandable. I hope you feel better after some rest."

"Thank you."

Of course, when I saw the new patient lying where Elaine had been, I knew rest would never be the cure for my illness. I could feel the need to see Elaine again, and for the first time I admitted that I cared, if nothing else. She had such a wonderful aura when she smiled, like the room became a little bit brighter. But that was long gone, it seemed. I was fooling myself, still thinking that there was some way that I could help her.

Still, the hours until lunch dragged on endlessly, although I hardly knew what to do with myself once it was there. I stood in my office dumbly, habit eventually winning out. My usual lunch place was nearby, at least, and perhaps once I was fed I could reason myself through this. Or so I hoped, but my reasoning was gone in an instant when I heard the argument happening toward the far corner of the restaurant.

"What did you say?" snapped an unattractively large man I presumed was the manager. He would have towered over most, making his aggressive posture all the more horrifying when I realized who he was intimidating.

"The treatment didn't work. I'm sorry to put in my resignation this way, but—"

"But what? Huh? I thought you were actually a decent worker, but you sure proved me wrong. You're just as worthless as the rest of them. Shouldn't be too hard to replace you, either," he added cruelly. His words visibly cut at Elaine, as she fought against tears.

"I'm sorry—"

"Don't you dare apologize," I snapped at her.

The words stunned me as much as the two arguing. I didn't know when I had stepped out of line, though next thing I realized I was standing beside Elaine in her wheelchair, wishing I stood even a few inches taller in the face of this behemoth.

"This is none of your business, Li," she hissed quietly.

"For once, she's right. Keep your nose out of this if you don't want it to get any flatter," he threatened. Despite my reactionary insult at his comment it was hard to resist the urge to get out of the way. Impossibly, I was more angered by his assault on Elaine's spirit than frightened.

What could I do against a giant? Bluff.

"Really, that's unnecessary," I snapped irritably, doing my best to channel my father. He could burn in hell and the devil himself wouldn't dare to treat him without respect. "We are in the presence of a woman, whom you've shamelessly verbally abused, no less. You will use your manners and you will *hold your tongue* when I am speaking," I added sharply as he made to protest.

"Now, I am the doctor treating Miss Crowley and her condition. She will return to work when I say she can, not a second sooner, and if I hear or see any more of this abusive and potentially damaging behavior directed at my patient—undoing my incredibly sensitive treatment—I will sue you for every penny I'm worth an hour that I've put into her care. Have I made myself clear?" I demanded, my legs weak with disbelief that I had mouthed off to this monster of a man. It seemed to have worked, though, as he reevaluated the situation.

He debated a moment before he sighed. "I'm sorry, Elaine, Doctor. I'll get back to work."

I nodded, keeping an eye on him until he had returned to the kitchen. I let out a shaky breath and smiled at Elaine. "I can't believe that worked."

She just stared at me for a long moment before blurting out, "I never thought you had the spine!"

"To be honest, I borrowed one for that," I confessed, laughing somewhat giddily. "Were you here for anything aside from getting into a bit of trouble?"

"Apparently, to get annoyed by a doctor. Why, what brings you here?" she retorted, wheeling herself toward the door. I opened it for her, following after her. "Come to weasel more money out of me?"

"No," I cried swiftly, startled she would think that. It hurt, I found. "No, actually, I—shouldn't you wait for your friend?" I asked as she started toward the sidewalk.

"Who's that?" she asked without looking.

"Whoever brought you here."

"Me, myself, and I," she replied dryly.

"Wait!" I called after her, and she finally stopped herself. "Let me take you home."

She started off again. "I like the scenery."

"Then let me walk you," I offered, catching up to her easily. She said nothing, giving me a solid glare. "Please."

"Really, what do you want from me?" she demanded, and I saw those tears starting again.

"I..." *Smile*. "I just want to help. Perhaps over some lunch?"

Elaine sighed heavily, shaking her head slowly. "I'm really not in the mood to discuss any of that medical crap right now."

"I don't want to, either," I told her honestly. I held my hands up in surrender. "I'm not a doctor, for the rest of the day. Just a regular guy."

"A regular guy...asking me out for lunch?" she turned it

around on me with a smirk. At least her eyes were drying from their tears.

Still, I couldn't help smiling. "Something like that."

Finally, she returned the smile. "I'm not sure why you're interested, but it's been a while since anyone's asked me."

"Is that a yes, then?"

"Yes, in a roundabout sort of way," she agreed easily. For a moment I saw her, the girl that had captured my attention without my realizing. "You can take me to lunch."

"Would you prefer to use a car or wa—" I stopped myself short. The only image I had of her in my mind was still the graceful beauty I had seen in those videos, despite the month of staring at the bitter truth. "I'm sorry."

She shrugged. "I'm fine. It takes some adjusting to, I know. All of my friends have been making the same slip of the tongue. I can't expect the world to change how it acts just for me."

"No, I—I suppose not," I agreed quietly, smiling at her. Wrong as it was that the car had hit her, I didn't think anyone else could have handled it with more dignity. "So, where would you like to go?"

Elaine stopped to think for a second. "Well, we only have about forty minutes left of your lunch break."

I couldn't help glancing at my watch, but she was right. For a moment, I found myself frustrated that, even when I was offering selflessly, she wouldn't accept it at face value. She didn't think of herself. No, she still thought of me and my schedule first.

"As I said, for the rest of the day I'm not a doctor, just Li," I told her firmly. Before she could ask or I had to admit my reasons to myself, I added, "I have a half-day today. They already know that I'm not coming back from lunch."

She smiled. "I'm glad you have some time off. You always work too much."

"Thank you. Your concern is noted, Doctor Crowley," I teased her, but I genuinely appreciated her noticing, that she thought I worked *too* hard, too *much*. My family would greatly disagree with her assessment. My father's favorite description of my work ethic was lazy and unprofessional, even as I worked my way to the top of my field.

"I'd advise medications, too, but most that I have in mind are illegal in some way or another," she added somberly, making me laugh. Her smile broadened. "I didn't know you knew how to laugh."

I nodded slowly, refusing to reply to her painfully attentive comment. "I'm buying and I'm driving. Where do you want to go?"

Stunned, Elaine stared at me for a long minute while she seemed to be considering something. "Why are you so insistent that you have lunch with me?"

"I want to get to know you," I admitted honestly, though that only seemed to upset her. For a brief moment, she seemed angry, almost heartbroken.

Despite what I saw, she put on a smile. "I'm not sure why, but all right, Just Li. There's a small café about two miles down the road from here. Do you think you can make it?"

"Is that a challenge, Elaine?" I asked with a confident smirk, leaning in to be sure that she'd heard me. It was only after I'd placed myself there that I realized how close I was and, for a moment, I had trouble not moving any closer.

If I'd thought she was attractive before, I hadn't been paying attention. Up close, she was breathtaking. Being able to see the exact curves of her well-rounded lips as the mottled light from the trees above played across her seemingly flawless skin. Despite how tempting her lips had become, it was her eyes that truly captured me, igniting a desire to do nothing more than stare into their depths.

"Maybe it is," she relented, looking in the direction of our destination. The break in eye contact freed me from my trance and I straightened quickly. She gave me a mischievous grin. "I wouldn't want to ruin your pride, though."

"Good luck with that. So far, no college April Fool's prank has come close to knocking me off of my high horse," I warned her, enjoying the look of determination that crossed her face. I reached around to the back of her wheelchair instinctively and began walking.

Before I knew it, Elaine had put on the breaks. "I can get myself there, thank you."

"I'm sorry," I apologized quickly, releasing my grip and stepping to her side again. "It's...force of habit."

Her smile took me by surprise. "I understand. I'm sorry for snapping, it's just...I'm not a cripple. I can take care of myself," she said firmly, although the way she said it made me wonder if she was trying to convince herself more than me.

"I know," I told her gently, watching her struggle with this for another minute. Unable to bear it any longer, I sought a distraction. "What's the name of this café of yours?"

<u>The Little Canary</u>

"Mother."

The sly older woman who had raised me didn't even acknowledge that I had spoken. "I've already discussed the benefits of this marriage with her parents. You're to meet each other within the month and begin courting her. Is that understood, Da?" she asked sternly, more commanding than seeking my consent.

But I nodded. This was my mother, and as my parents' only son I had to think of the future of our family. "I understand, Mother."

"Good."

~~ * ~ * ~ * ~~

I couldn't help thinking of my own mother as Elaine told me about her family on the way to her favorite café, The Little Canary. Her father had passed away eleven years ago, during his service in the military. She was thirteen; her twin sisters were both only two. Her mother had barely kept herself together long enough to get Elaine to her fifteenth birthday. Not a month later, she had a job and took over caring for her little sisters.

"I'm sorry," I said quietly, unsure of how to address such a delicate topic. I had never genuinely associated with anyone who had come from such a tragic background.

"Thank you, but I don't need any pity," she told me bluntly.

I bristled at her brush off. "Then why did you tell me all of this?"

"You're the one who wanted to get to know me, remember?" she scoffed at my reaction. "I just told you what happened, like you asked. It's over and done, I don't want pity even if it comes with a

15

thousand dollars attached."

"Beggars can't be choosers, I thought." The words escaped me before I had time to regret thinking them.

"Neither can asshats, but you don't see me pointing that out," she retorted patiently. In an instant, I'd proven to be inconsiderate and receive verbal punishment from a woman. Between the two of us, I had been damn well put in my place.

I stopped myself and sighed. "You're right. I'm sorry, that was very rude of me."

"Yes, it was," she replied somewhat sharply. "But your apology's accepted, Li. Thank you."

Her words did little to appease my chagrin, instead reigniting the times my words had effectively sentenced her to death. "Why do you thank me like that?"

"Like what?"

"I've just wronged you," I told her earnestly, loathing the feeling that I *had* wronged her, so terribly, so many times I was beginning to lose count.

"But you just apologized," she said slowly, and I could see that my argument was confusing her somehow.

I sighed quietly to myself. "Never mind it."

She shrugged, diverting from the path suddenly. My eyes followed her for a moment as she wheeled herself toward a quaint store at the end of a shopping complex. I started after her briskly, catching up easily. As she struggled up the nearest ramp, I went ahead to hold the door for her.

"You don't have to do that," she grumbled quietly.

"Open a door for a lady?" She shot me a glare I happily smiled at. "It's only manners, I promise. I have to save face somehow."

She debated a moment longer before she accepted the gesture. "Thank you. Welcome to The Little Canary, by the way."

I breathed in deeply, the smell of freshly brewed teas and coffees intermingled with that of baked goods, making the aroma all the more intoxicating to my senses. The gentleman behind the counter recognized Elaine, his face lighting up with a smile.

"Elaine! Good to see you after your accident. Finally," he added begrudgingly, but he couldn't seem to cover the joy in his voice. As he spoke, a small woman came from the back of the store, relieved as Elaine came into her view. Before she could speak, the small woman's eyes fell on me and she did a double-take as her face broke out in a grin.

"Oh, Ellie, who's this?" she asked, voice hushed.

"Ellie?" I echoed. To my surprise, she blushed as she looked back at me.

"Carl, Jane, this is Doctor Li. Li, this is Carl and Jane, they own The Canary," she introduced us, shy for the first time I could recall. Was she embarrassed? Of me?

Carl gave me a sunny smile that warmed up the room. "Welcome to The Little Canary, Li. Make yourself at home."

<u>**Audition**</u>

When Carl had invited me to be at home, I never imagined that I could, or would. After all, the somewhat bohemian café was not someplace anyone of my class would be willingly seen. Perhaps as some charity act for publicity, but that I was enjoying afternoons of leisure there was breaking a list of taboos.

It had only been two weeks since I'd taken Elaine to lunch, and already it felt as though I had frequented this place for years. The Canary was always warm when I entered, Carl or Jane waiting behind the counter or lounging comfortably with their customers. When I walked in after work today, however, there was no one else present.

Carl looked up from reading his newspaper, waving at me in greeting. "Good evening, Li. How was work?"

"Mostly paperwork today, but it went well, thank you, Carl," I replied politely as I took a seat. "Has it been empty all day?"

Carl nodded. "It usually is toward the middle of the week."

"Ah." I pulled out the notes I had been compiling for the procedures that could help Elaine. Slipping on my reading glasses, I glanced over the first few pages before the doorbell rang as someone entered. I peered over the top of my glasses; I couldn't help smiling. "Hello, Elaine."

She wheeled up next to me, looking at my assortment of papers inquisitively. "Hey, Li."

"How are you?" I asked, trying to see past her calm demeanor to understand if she truly was better or worse today. Seeing her so frequently, I did enjoy being able to monitor her condition outside of a controlled environment.

Elaine smiled, hiding something from me. "Fine, as I've been telling you for the last two weeks."

Something's wrong. I couldn't shake the feeling, even as Jane came out to adore her, sitting with us and chattering about people I didn't know and places I hadn't heard of. I forced my eyes to look back at my pages even if I couldn't focus on reading, just to stop myself staring. What was wrong? Elaine had been doing so well.

"What are you reading, Li?" asked Elaine, pulling me from the worry for a moment. She smiled for me, the expression lighting her face briefly.

I smiled back. Now was as good a time as any. "Research notes."

"What for?" Her curiosity added a certain element that made her...adorable, I decided.

"Stem cell therapies to treat spinal injuries," I replied calmly. She had to know sooner or later. After all, I would need her permission before I could help her.

She fell silent for a long time. When I looked up, she had tears in her eyes, glistening there like diamonds. "One of your patients?"

I nodded slowly, keeping my eyes on hers as I replied quietly, "Her treatments with me didn't go very well, so I'm trying to find a way to help her."

"So she's got to be pretty well off, to afford extra treatments like that," she forced out, but I heard her choking on the words.

I tried to smile for her, wanting to tell her that I hadn't given up. She would dance again. "Honestly, I'm not sure how well off she is, but I don't care. No matter how much it is, I'll pay it to see her made better."

"Like there's something *wrong* with me? There's nothing wrong with me!" she yelled at me, moving away as quickly as she could. She looked angry and hurt, so far from the vibrant woman I remembered first meeting.

I watched after her, worried. "I just want to help."

"I don't need your help!" she yelled, the tears brimming over and spilling across her cheeks. She glared at me before making for the door. "And you know what? I don't want it, either!"

When the door slammed behind her, I found myself balanced between anger and grief. The papers in my hand mocked me; I tossed them to the coffee table in front of me. Carl and Jane were simply there, eyes downcast not in shame but disappointment.

"You're letting her leave like that?" I demanded, as much out of myself as I did of them. Something was wrong for Elaine, yet we all merely sat there doing nothing.

Jane shrugged and sighed, obviously defeated. "Her mother did the same thing when Elaine's father passed away: found the bottom of a bottle and screamed until we all went away."

"She's *drunk*?" Neither of them answered, but it was enough. I stood abruptly, turning for the door and keeping my pace brisk. The evening air was beginning to nip at me as I searched for either Elaine or any sign of where she had gone. When I spotted her, it felt as though the world was taunting her and forcing me to watch.

Not a hundred feet from The Canary, Elaine's wheel had caught on a pothole, laying on its side now with the poor woman thrown from the seat a couple of feet away. I made my way over, cringing as I came into earshot, listening to her crying in misery. She was faced away, so I stood still for a full minute, unsure of what to do next. Finally, after I had listened to enough of her grief, I reached out and righted her chair, startling her. She whipped around quickly, propping herself up on her elbows as she glared at me.

"What do *you* want?" she demanded angrily, but I saw a flash of fear cross her face. "Why won't you leave me alone?!"

I knelt silently, offering my arms to help her up again. She made to slap me away but I grabbed her wrist to stop her. She struggled to free herself, all but thrashing before I pulled her close and held her tight to keep her from harming herself. She screamed in frustration, biting me, fighting against my grip.

"It's okay. Elaine, it's okay, you can calm down now," I told her gently and quietly, relieved when it actually worked. I barely remembered any of my mandatory psychology classes anymore, now wishing I'd paid more attention. "Good. That's good, Elaine, thank you."

She shrunk in on herself, sobbing. "It's not fair. It was today. I was so close—It isn't fair..."

"I know, Elaine," I agreed regretfully, nodding slowly. "I know. That's why I want to help. I want to see you made better."

"I had an audition today." She trembled in my arms, struggling to collect herself. "I got the letter the day of my...the day that I...Why did it have to be me?"

I didn't know how to answer or if I could. I barely understood what I was doing there anymore, how it was I was sitting in an empty parking lot with a crippled woman weeping in my arms. All I had wanted was to understand why her friends loved and adored her so much. Understanding led to wanting to help her led to needing to...what?

What did I need from her?

"You'll get another chance," I told her, unable to speak much more over a whisper. Her fingers latched onto my shirt tightly as she seemed to wither into me. "I promise you, Elaine. I'll help you walk again, help you dance. I want nothing more than to see you dance," I added before realizing just how true that was. There really was nothing else I wanted more than that distant imagining of seeing her dance.

She was too far gone in her drunken tears, the taste of cheap beer still heavy on her breath as she sobbed. Again, I wished I knew what to do, but I had never cared enough to learn before. Just a few movies I had glanced at while my sister had watched, but...

How did those scenes go? How did the male lead make these things into happy endings? Why did this hurt me and what could I do to end it?

All I could think of was getting her out of the cold air, hugging her more tightly and rubbing her back as I braced myself to lift her. She seemed to be quieting, but when I looked her tears were still running freely. I brushed away some of her tears, ducking my face to give her a peck on the forehead.

"You're going to be fine," I told her firmly, wrapping one arm around her shoulder and the other around her limp knees. When I lifted her I was surprised by how light she was, how effortless it was to walk back to The Canary with her still cradled in my arms. She kept her eyes trained on me, her grip tight as ever with her fingers curled into a fist against my chest.

As I approached the door, Jane saw me coming and opened it for me. I entered the warm atmosphere gladly, taking a seat on a sofa. Elaine was still halfway in my lap and bundled in my arms, her useless legs stretched out beside us. I couldn't help staring at her in the light, so close yet so far away as her eyes gazed past me into some unknown distance. After a minute, I came back to myself.

"Her chair—"

"Carl's got it," interrupted Jane, appearing at my side with a steaming mug. I took it readily, propping Elaine against me before offering her the tea. She sipped at it before allowing her head to fall against my shoulder with a tired sigh, fading out quickly.

"Thank you, Jane." I kept rubbing her arms, her back, holding her cooler hands between my warmer ones.

Jane simply stared at me for a long moment. "I should be thanking you. A decade and a half, I've never seen Elaine like this with anyone. I don't think I've ever seen her genuinely trust someone before."

How was it I seemed to keep losing my words this evening? Was there a lack of anything to say? Of course, if that were true...

"She still doesn't trust me," I replied quietly, surprised by how greatly this disappointed me.

Jane gave me a gentle smile. "She's getting there, Li. Just give her a little more time, she'll see what we do."

I looked up at her in curiosity, finding myself hopeful and excited by the idea of Elaine—now asleep in my arms—trusting me. "Do you think so?"

She nodded. "You're the man we've all been hoping for, Li. Just promise me something?"

"Yes?"

"Take care of her."

~~ * ~ * ~ * ~~

"Li?"

I looked up at Elaine, smiling when I took in her own happiness. "What is it, Elaine?"

She paused for a moment before a light blush tinted her cheeks. "Can we talk? Elsewhere?"

"Of course." I set aside my paperwork, motioning to Carl for him to keep an eye on it. Elaine made for the door. I opened it for her and followed after her. "What do you need, Elaine?"

She stopped herself at the sidewalk, her blush growing darker with her next words, "Would you, um...Would you walk me to the park?"

I had to take a moment to process what she had said. "I...Elaine?"

"Well, I think I'm okay with that now," she said shyly, keeping her head down. Without questioning her any further, I stepped behind her chair and started walking us towards the park down the street. This was nice, certainly peaceful, and it felt wonderful to know that she was comfortable enough with me that she allowed me to help her.

Despite how blissful this was, however, I had to know. "What did you want to talk about?"

"I was thinking..." She stopped herself as she looked out toward a particularly serene grove of trees. "Can we go over there? Please?"

"Whatever you'd like," I told her sincerely. I brought us up alongside a park bench and took a seat beside her with a quiet sigh. Still, this was one of the times I was coming to cherish with Elaine, slowing down and taking a moment to breathe in the world instead of life rushing by. "Is this good for you?"

"Yes, thank you." Her voice was filled with emotion as she stared ahead of us at the playground. A long minute passed before she finally looked back to me with pleading eyes. "I...I'm sorry for how I've been acting. I know you're just trying to help, and I'd like to let you. I mean, what happened last week...Li..."

"Don't apologize," I found myself pleading with her. "Please. You were only upset, and I was happy to help you. It's something I've been hoping to do for some time now."

That stopped her short, bringing a smile to her lips and tears to her eyes. "Thank you, Li. For everything. Especially last week, with what happened. You...I never thought that anyone could care that much," she admitted to me. I could see how difficult it was for her. She was trembling fiercely in her chair, unable to meet my gaze anymore. What could I do? I hated seeing her like this.

"Elaine." Her eyes met mine, and for a moment the world stood still as I took in the grace of her features. In an instant, I knew I was going to regret this but I couldn't stop myself. Elaine's eyes drew me in as I ducked my head to press my lips to hers.

For a moment, I had enough awareness to detest this for the mistake it was, to remember that I was already betrothed to the daughter of a far wealthier family. But then, why should I care? How could I, when I had the most remarkable woman here?

I pulled back, enjoying how darkly her cheeks had flushed. "I suppose that sums up most of it."

She nodded slowly. "What sums up the rest?"

I smiled and leaned in again for a longer kiss that lingered even after I pulled back. My eyes never left hers, my words soft, "I will see you dance again, Elaine. And it will be the happiest moment of my life."

Elaine stared at me intently, smiling slowly so that her lips curved upward. The words escaped her as a quiet breath nearly lost on the breeze, "Thank you, Li."

The Calm

"When do her treatments start?"

"Today," I replied, the tension in my voice surprising Mark. He stared at me, confused. I sighed. "That's where we're going, Mark, to pick her up."

He nodded. "It's about time I met this girl you've been telling me about."

"You are coming to drive us back to her house, *not* meet her," I interjected firmly, two exits away now. Irrational excitement had me shaking, unable to wait until I saw Elaine. As if one treatment would miraculously heal her. "That you two are near one another at all is purely coincidental."

He watched me for a long moment. "Why am I driving?"

"So that I can sit with Elaine and see how she's doing, after..." I slowed for the red light, the medical building coming into view. I had seen it a hundred times, never taking a second glance at it before. "There it is."

"Don't you think it's risky, treating your not-girlfriend at your fiancée's father's building?" asked Mark as we parked. "Not mentioning you picking her up yourself. What if you're recognized?"

I unbuckled, pulling on a hooded jacket and flipping the hood up before I left the car. I met Mark around the other side. "They have the best doctors for what she needs."

"I don't think I've ever seen you take risks like this before." As if realizing he'd almost sounded concerned, he added, "You look like you're going to rob the place."

His initial comment startled me, because he was right. I never took a risk, especially not like this. For Elaine, I was putting my reputation and, as a result, my career on the line. From there, my entire family's name was at stake.

All for one woman.

But it was too late for me to reply to his comment—that he was right, and she likely didn't understand fully what my actions meant.

We entered the building, looking somewhat out of place among the well-dressed people here. I had come in a pair of old jeans and hooded sweatshirt, hair disheveled, intending to have my chances of being recognized lessened. After the initial shock of my appearance, everyone turned away to ignore my presence. Good. This was just what I needed.

"Good afternoon," greeted the desk clerk with a forced smile, her eyes judging me in an instant. "How may I assist you, sir?"

"I'm here to pick up a patient," I told her quietly.

"Name?"

"I'm sorry?"

"Of the patient, sir," she explained rather forcefully.

"Elaine Crowley." My throat was nearly choking me, I was so anxious. Was she all right? Could anyone recognize me? What would happen to her if they did?

The clerk paid me no mind, typing away on her keyboard for a moment. She finally looked up at me with another false smile. "She's just been released. Please take a seat, we'll have a nurse bring her out."

"Thank you." I made my way to the seating area, but I couldn't sit. Instead, I found myself pacing impatiently, back and forth as my thoughts bit at me.

Mark watched me for a minute. "I think you'd better stop before you wear a hole through the floor."

I turned on him to tell him off, stopping halfway when I saw Elaine emerging from behind a pair of manicured doors. I noticed the embarrassment on her face, then the man pushing her chair.

"Oh, Elaine," I sighed, by her chair faster than I thought I could ever move. The man stepped back as I approached. My hand brushed her cheek, her face lighting up as I took over wheeling her towards the desk clerk.

"Do you have your next appointment scheduled, Miss Crowley?" asked the clerk kindly. Elaine nodded tiredly. "Good. Take care, any of your questions can be answered by reading the information in the folder the doctor gave you."

"Thank you," I replied, going for the door. I heard the chatter of people behind me, but that no longer mattered, nor did my risk of being recognized. I had to get Elaine home to rest. The world could wait.

I made it to the car before I realized that Mark wasn't behind me. His figure was still distinguishable behind the broad glass windows of the medical office. I sighed heavily.

"What's taking you, Mark?" I muttered, opening the back door of the car. Elaine stared at me groggily for a long moment, then the car, then back at me. "Are you all right?"

She shook her head. "No."

I was on my knee in an instant, taking in her condition. "What is it? What's wrong, Elaine?"

"I think I need help getting in the car," she confessed, frowning. I almost laughed in my relief, smiling and nodding.

"Okay. Okay, I can help with that," I told her gently. A few minutes later, I had settled her into the car and stored her wheelchair in the trunk.

Mark appeared suddenly, looking rather pleased with himself. "All right. Are we ready to go?"

"Yes." I buckled in next to Elaine in the backseat, waiting until we were in motion to introduce them. "Elaine?"

"Yes, Li?" she moaned, turning a sleepy smile on me.

"I would like you to meet a good friend of mine, his name is Mark." I motioned to where he sat driving and she waved. "Mark, this is Elaine."

~~ * ~ * ~ * ~~

"Is this the right place?"

27

I checked the map and nodded. "Yes, that's it."

Mark pulled up, giving me a look of horror as he put the car in park. "Are you *sure* you don't want to take her back to your place? I mean, this looks like it should be condemned..."

My hand shot forward to smack his shoulder, his feigned injury still bringing me satisfaction. I turned to Elaine, stopping short when I saw how happily she slept, nestled into her seat and using my sweater as a pillow. The sigh left me unintentionally, drawing Mark's attention despite how quiet it was.

"Is she asleep?" he asked in a hushed tone. I nodded. "All right. I'll get the door, you carry her."

I wouldn't have had it any other way. I got out and went around to Elaine's door, waiting until Mark had gotten someone to answer the front door. I recognized Elaine's mother, heavy-set and still in her pajamas. Sighing to myself, I reached in and lifted Elaine out. She shifted in my arms, taking my shoulder to replace the sweater as her pillow.

"Shh, shh," I hushed her quietly, hoping that she could stay asleep. She needed to rest, my poor Elaine.

"About time she's back!" called her mother, leaving the doorway to move deeper into the elderly trailer home. I winced, but Elaine seemed completely at ease.

Mark entered ahead of me. I walked up the ramp to the porch easily before making my own cautious entry. My initial impression was the smell: an overpowering mixture of smoke, body odors, and aged foods nearly choking me. It took me a moment to adjust, finally taking in the mess. There was enough of a pathway for Elaine's chair to maneuver through the house, the rest an array of items that had simply collected and been shoved into piles together.

"Ignore the mess. Elaine hasn't been herself lately, slacking on the chores." Her mother's initially aggressive statement petered off to a careless murmur, "Damn girl..."

I looked at Elaine's sleeping face, and I understood more of why she was sad after her family visited her in the hospital. Manners won out, and I bit back any comments as I asked, "Where is her room, Ms. Crowley? Elaine fell asleep on the drive."

"Follow the hall, she's at the end," came her grumbled reply, refusing to look away from her television program.

Mark was obviously upset, making no effort to hide it as he muttered, "We shouldn't leave her here. I have a spare bedroom, Li."

I made my way down the hall a bit before I replied, just as quietly, "We also have dinner with my family, tonight of all nights."

"Well, take her with us, then," continued Mark determinedly.

"No, Mark." I shook my head slowly, opening the room at the end of the hall. The sight inside made me smile, the mess and disgrace of the rest of the house forced out by some magic. The brightly colored walls were covered with posters of ballerinas, dancers, artworks from all styles and genres

Pictures of Elaine and her friends were centered around her bed. I stepped across the room, pulling back the covers to tuck her into bed. She began to stir, staring up at me tiredly.

"Hi, Li," she yawned quietly.

"Hey." I smiled for her, brushing the hair from her face. "How do you feel?"

She moaned. "Sore. Tired."

"That's normal, Elaine." I nodded, taking her hand and giving it a squeeze. Behind me, I heard Mark muttering to himself. I glanced back in time to see him dropping off her chair and medical folder before excusing himself. "Just get some rest. I'm going to be back to check on you tomorrow."

"Where are you going?" The question was strained, no matter how calmly she was trying to act.

"I have something I need to do tonight," I told her, feeling strangely guilty. "If I could cancel it, Elaine, you know I would."

"Really?" she mumbled, drifting off again.

"In a heartbeat." She was asleep already. I gave her a peck on the cheek before I stood. As I did, I caught sight of a photo of the inside of The Canary which startled me. The photo was of myself, reading through my files. It gave me pause; my smile broadened unexpectedly. "Sleep well, Elaine."

29

<u>Brace</u>

"She has what?" asked Mark in shock.

"A picture of me." I couldn't help a grin, straightening my jacket in front of the closet mirror. My custom suit accented my form smartly, making me look more like a businessman than a doctor. Perfect for my family's weekly dinner. "There we are."

"You two are adorable together," he laughed, pulling his jacket on. He sighed heavily. "That house, though...I still can't believe that we *left* her there!"

I shut my closet door with more force than was necessary, making both of us jump. "I had to, Mark, you know that. I can't be bringing random women to my house, especially a patient—"

"*Ex*-patient, my friend, and now that there's pictures involved, she's definitely not random," he interjected firmly.

"I'm engaged!"

"Oh, right, what would the future Mrs. Li think?" he sighed, exasperated. "You two have already started kissing! You're going to have to come clean sooner or later."

"It was just the once, and I know!" I snapped. But his words wounded me deeply. For no other reason than inciting the thought of saying goodbye to Elaine, because there was no way for me to back away from this arranged marriage. I took a deep breath and sighed, nodding slowly. "I know, Mark. I'm sorry, I can't...I just need more time, until she's well again. I'll stop this, but I need to see that she'll be okay. I just want to take care of her."

He shook his head slowly. "If you say so, Li. It sounds like a lot more than professional concern, though."

It is. "Professional concern? That's all it is."

"Maybe, if you say it enough, it'll come true," teased Mark, heading for the door. I didn't argue, well aware that whatever I could say in my defense would be a lie. Whatever I felt or wanted was irrelevant right now. The best I could do was help Elaine and make a silent exit from her life later.

We left for dinner in his brazen red sports car, the engine purring smoothly as we raced down the freeway toward downtown. Our silence was an overbearing companion for the first stretch of the drive until Mark finally broke it.

"Are either of you, I don't know, grateful?" he asked thoughtfully, the question startling me after the previous quiet. Mark glanced over at me, clarifying, "For the accident, I mean."

I scoffed, nearly insulted by the question. "Why would I ever be grateful for *that*?"

"Well, without it, Elaine wouldn't have missed her audition. She would have left and you never would have known what you were missing," he explained, giving me a stab of guilt. Because, yet again, he was so very right. Elaine's accident seemed to be one of the best things to have ever happened to me, as cruel as that thought was. Without it, I may never have truly met her, and that thought hit me with surprising force.

"You're right," I told him somberly, forcing the knot from my throat. I hated myself then, that it took her losing hope for her life's dreams for me to see what an amazing woman Elaine was to start with. I sighed, my heart twisting in my chest.

Mark was quiet for a minute before saying what I'd known from the very beginning—what I'd known and *denied*. "As soon as her treatments kick in, you're going to have to leave her, Li. Fast, before your mother finds out."

I nodded slowly, my eyes burning with the grief I refused to shed. "I know."

~~ * ~ * ~ * ~~

"Well, that wasn't so bad," I sighed tiredly, stepping inside my house. Behind me, I heard Mark's car pulling away from the front steps and back down the driveway. Suddenly, I was all too aware of how lonely my empty house was, and how much I wished Elaine could be there with me. I slipped off my jacket and hung it in the closet, stopping there.

I couldn't move, caught up in the feeling of yearning for more than this lonely room. With a heavy sigh, I sat down on my bed and pulled out my cell phone. I stared down at it for a long moment before I searched for Elaine's contact information, a picture of her smiling face lighting up my screen. I couldn't help my smile, calling her. My foot tapped impatiently, heart pounding in my throat as I waited for her to answer. It rang once, twice, three times...four...

"Mm, Li?" Elaine's sleepy moan over the phone made me far happier than it should have.

I laughed quietly. "I'm sorry, Elaine, did I wake you up? Should I let you continue sleeping?"

She sounded much more alert as she replied, "Oh, no, you didn't wake me up! I've been awake for a while, actually, I've just been...reading."

She was such a terrible liar! "All right, I'm glad, Elaine. How are you feeling?"

"Ugh," she sighed, the sound of her shifting scuffling over the phone noisily. "Like my head was hit by a ton of bricks and then packed with cotton. But my back isn't hurting too bad, so that's good, I guess."

"I've heard that's normal, but I'm sorry for your discomfort," I replied, feeling surprisingly awkward and nervous as we sat in silence for a long moment before she replied at all.

"Li?"

"Yes, Elaine?"

"I'm glad you called," she told me, voice trembling slightly. Was she nervous, as well? "I missed you."

Like that, my heart filled to the point of bursting with happiness. She missed me? Like I missed her in this empty house? How was I supposed to respond? Mark was right earlier, after all. I was going to have to let Elaine go before my mother found out about her and had a chance to attack her somehow.

But I wanted desperately to indulge in this relationship. It was so easy to be with her, my initial curiosity having turned into affection that needed to be shown and acted upon. It felt as though—if it wasn't nurtured—it would turn to excruciating pain in my chest.

And yet...

"You should get some sleep, Elaine," I replied in a murmur, grimacing and regretting the choice of words immediately. This had gone too far already. She deserved so much better. "I'll check on you in the morning?"

Why was that a question?

"Oh. Yeah, I guess..." The disappointment in her tone was painfully clear. "Goodnight, Li."

"Goodnight, Ellie."

The Storm

"Oh, my gosh, Li?!"

Oh, hell.

I spun on my heel, lost for a course of action as I was torn between the impulse to flee and the need to stand my ground and wait for Elaine to be released. I was only five minutes early. Five minutes! What were the chances *she* would be here?

In the end, I settled for trying to smooth things over nonchalantly, "Annette! Lovely to see you."

The replying grin from my petite fiancée was that of a madwoman. "What are you doing here?! I thought you were a busy hotshot doctor or something."

Or something? "Surgeon. And I am, I'm just here on behalf of a patient."

"Really? Which one? For how long?" Her obsessively inquisitive nature was nothing short of grating.

"That's all confidential." Goodness, gracious, we were going to be married! Couldn't she allow me what little freedom I had left?

"Right, right," she sighed, smiling with humor at her own ditziness. I couldn't believe this was an heiress to an empire. "I hope they're improving, at least. Daddy takes pride in his medical centers."

"I'm aware," I replied dryly. I pursed my lips. Annette was being an admittedly good sport about my overall detachment regarding our engagement. Perhaps a small bone thrown her way wouldn't hurt? "She is, actually. Improving, that is."

"Oh, that's great!" She grinned with such earnest fervor, I wondered how she didn't drive herself crazy. "Just remember to make time for our wedding planning sessions, too."

"If my schedule allows it," I agreed reluctantly. Then again, I *was* extremely busy these days. She couldn't exactly plan our wedding without me entirely, could she? It was certainly a tempting notion to see how long I could delay things.

"Sir? Miss Crowley is being discharged now," called the receptionist at the desk.

I smiled politely, realizing with a flash of panic that I needed to dismiss Annette so that I could discreetly handle the transaction for this appointment. Thinking quickly, I decided to take advantage of her overly helpful nature and simply make it up to Elaine later.

"Annette, I need to handle her paperwork for a moment. Would you mind checking on El—Miss Crowley for me?" I caught myself quickly, but I could still feel this charade unraveling with every word I spoke.

"Sure!" She bounced off as Elaine was brought into the waiting area. I watched her closely, waiting to see that she had taken the bait and was fully engaged in introductions with Elaine.

Hurrying through the payment of the appointment, I felt a heavy weight settling over me. This was too close. This was flirting dangerously with discovery. Mark was right. I *needed* to stop this. Elaine was ready to start physical therapy soon if she hadn't already today. I stared at the empty line that needed my signature, that realization hitting me harder with every passing second.

It was time for me to go.

"Sir?"

I signed hurriedly, finishing the transaction and feeling like I had just finished a marathon. My heart and lungs were aching from the strain of keeping my composure. I turned back to the women chatting near the exit. Poor Elaine looked exhausted, and I was certain that Annette wasn't helping.

"Hey, Li," greeted Elaine tiredly when I approached.

I smiled carefully. "How are you feeling?"

She shrugged. "Like I just did the start of a montage."

"Well, I should get you home to rest, then. Annette, thank you, it was good to see you."

"Oh, I was happy to help! You just feel better soon, okay?" she told Elaine with a friendly smile. Annette waved farewell as I stepped behind Elaine, wheeling her out of the building. As much as I had yearned for relief, that heavy weight didn't leave me as I left the office. Something had clicked, and there wasn't anything I could do to change it back.

"Annette was very sweet. I hope we see her next time."

There were so many things I needed to address in that innocent comment. Where could I hope to start? As I opened the front passenger door for Elaine, I looked into the face of the woman I had so desperately wanted to help. She was smiling. It was genuine, too, and hopeful. Elaine was *hopeful*.

"Oh, I started physical therapy today," she told me excitedly.

Not today, I decided in an instant. Helping her into the car, I knew I had to talk to her—tell her, and soon—but not today. Elaine was getting better, and she was hopeful. We'd both worked too hard to help her reach this point, and I wouldn't ruin it now.

Soon, just not today.

Aftershock

Not today.

Today was Carl's and Jane's anniversary. Somehow, every day these last two weeks had some reason the timing wasn't right. Mark was pressuring me more every day now, especially since Annette had made a point to check in about Elaine at a dinner with our parents. I'd managed to deter her curiosity from anything more than a curt reply, but everything was still escalating. Too quickly, and too dangerously for Elaine's best interests.

Still, not today.

"I wish I could find someone and have what you two have," commented Carol, nudging Jane with a finger.

Harry was indignant at the comment. "Hey! Sitting right here, Carol."

"I know." She grinned, continuing with teasing him as the celebrations unfolded in the Canary.

Elaine leaned over toward me, mumbling, "I think I liked them best when I had morphine on demand."

I nearly choked on my drink as I fought the impulse to spit it out through my laughter. I turned a playfully shocked smirk on her. The radiant glee on her face was a relief. She had been improving almost daily since she'd started physical therapy, even if she still needed the wheelchair for now. She was happy and hopeful again, so much more like the woman I remembered before the accident.

"Li? What are you staring at?" asked Elaine. I couldn't help noticing how adorable she was when she smiled. I shouldn't have been thinking about her lips past the most basic observations, but it was hard to resist when she was this happy.

I shrugged. "You look well, is all."

"Right." She rolled her eyes. "That's why you've been acting funny lately, huh?"

I smiled tightly. I'd hoped I had been more discreet with my inner turmoils. "Elaine, you know—"

My reply was cut off by the jingle of The Canary's door. My attention strayed out of curiosity before it froze in horror. I stood out of ingrained habit, eyes wide as I realized fully what this new guest meant.

"Mother."

Elaine craned her neck to look. "Wait, what?"

My mother's expression was severe as she took in the quaint cafe with disdain. "*This* is where you're assisting a patient, Da?"

"For private consultations," I offered weakly, knowing the excuse was thin. We were in the middle of a public celebration, after all.

Please, not today.

Jane made to greet her new patron warmly, "Welcome to The Little Canary. It's so wonderful to meet you!"

Mother stared through the peaceful offering coolly. "I'm here to collect my son."

"Oh." Elaine glanced my way worriedly. "Li, is everything okay?"

I nodded curtly. "Let me grab my notes, Mother. I'll be out shortly."

"Yes, you will," agreed Mother dryly. She spared the shop and its occupants one last look of scathing disappointment before she stalked to the car out front. Her driver helped her into the back.

"Whoa. What was *that*?" wondered Carl, joining us after collecting a fresh tray of baked goods from the back.

"I need to go." I hoped the statement wasn't as final as it felt. There was very little for me to collect, but I took my time with it. I wasn't ready. "I'm sorry for the disruption."

Not today.

"Li, is everything okay?" Jane asked Elaine's earlier question concernedly.

Cinderella Dances

I hesitated, my bag full of notes feeling too heavy in my hands. No, everything was not okay, but I wasn't entirely sure how much was *wrong*, either. It must have seemed odd, how quickly I responded to my mother's beckoning, but...

If she knew about Elaine, there was far more at stake now than whatever opinions they had of me.

"I'm sorry, I need to go," I said again, fighting the impulse to look at Elaine. I didn't want to see her upset. I wasn't sure I could make myself leave if I knew how distressed she was. Without looking back, I made my way to the door.

"Li?"

I stopped at the door, turning back just enough to let her know that I was listening. I could hear the stress in her voice. This shouldn't be how things ended, whatever it was. But I couldn't shake the feeling of how final it all seemed.

"I'll see you later?"

She knew, too, didn't she? It wouldn't have been a question otherwise. I cringed at that thought. Why did this cut so deeply? It wasn't anything serious, right? That's what I'd been telling Mark. I only wanted to see her dance.

Not today, I realized regretfully.

"I need to go."

No matter how calloused I had been considered in previous years, I didn't realize how deeply I could loathe that trait until the ring of the door's bell echoed in my ears. How could I let those be my last words to Elaine? I hoped I would have the opportunity to rectify the mistake, but I knew that was wishful thinking. Mother wouldn't be here without good reason.

Turn around, I begged my body. My path stayed rooted toward the car Mother was in. *Please, don't let me leave it like this.*

My hand was on the door handle to the back seat, and I set my jaw firmly. Elaine's treatment was at risk, in so many ways right now. It would be selfish to do anything that might endanger it further. I had already failed her once. No matter how badly I wanted to hold on to these last months, I'd always known it would be temporary. I'd

39

just hoped it didn't have to end yet.

Not today, please.

I was barely buckled before the car was moving. Mother glared at me coldly from the seat beside me. I fought to keep my composure. There was no way she didn't know.

"How could you, Da?"

"Let me explain—"

"Explain what?" she demanded icily. "Did you think you could get away with this?"

"I was helping a patient!" I protested, regretting the outburst immediately. Arguing wasn't wise right now. My actions didn't need to be defended. My priority had to remain Elaine's continued treatment.

"She was discharged months ago, Da," she pointed out sharply.

"Yes," I agreed, submitting to the circumstances I had helped create. "She had a promising career in the performing arts. I considered it a charity case."

"An *expensive* charity case," snapped Mother, tossing a photo in my lap. I was kissing Elaine's forehead in the image. Harmless enough, if so much weren't at stake. "I've spoken to Annette, and she's happy to overlook all of this as pre-marital nervousness if you cease immediately."

"I will," I agreed quietly. Would she notice if I kept the photo? I didn't have anything from Elaine. I wanted proof that she had existed at all. "But Elaine's treatment—"

Mother's glare turned frigid. "What about it?"

"Please, Mother, she was an amazing dancer," I begged my case, hoping that my quick cooperation might help my attempt at bargaining. "I only ever wanted to help her continue her career. She's responding to treatment; she may even recover the ability to perform."

She pursed her lips, considering my pleas. She reached over and grabbed the photo. The sound of it ripping was painful to my ears. "Very well. I wouldn't want to insult your fiancée's family by wasting their hard work. But this charity case nonsense ends as of now. You'll change numbers, you'll change habits—even your home or work if you must. What you will not do is endanger this marriage, or your father will be informed of this in its entirety. I don't want to lose my son," she added with a hint of maternal concern that felt out of place.

"Whatever changes I have to make, I'll start today," I agreed eagerly. At least her treatment would continue. I hesitated a moment. "Elaine still can't drive herself."

"I will oversee the details." Mother dismissed my concern apathetically. "As I said, I don't want to insult our future in-laws' work. I don't want to hear another word on the topic, either."

I nodded in agreement, continuing the remainder of the ride in silence. Before I knew it, we were pulling into my home's driveway. My mother held out one hand expectantly, and I understood without further prompting. She was going to send someone to pick up my car. I passed her my keys, silently leaving the car and making my way to the house.

Putting in the door code, I stepped inside before I allowed myself to begin feeling what happened.

I breathed a tentative sigh of relief. Elaine would still be taken care of. That's what mattered. That's all that mattered. I could ignore the imposing loneliness of my barren home, knowing that. I could ignore the heavy pain in my chest because Elaine would dance again.

Not today, but soon enough.

My pocket blared with noise suddenly, startling me at first before I remembered my cell phone. I pulled it out, expecting Mark, and stared at the name with the sinking realization of what I'd bargained for.

I couldn't answer. It was Elaine, and all I could do was stare at her contact photo while her ringtone jingled on. I was angry, at no one in particular. I couldn't blame my mother: she was only looking out for my best interests. I'd dug us all into this hole. It was my fault. I wanted to see her dance, and I'd taken it too far.

The ringing stopped. I wasn't sure if that was better or worse as the following silence pressed in on me. This hurt. Physically, and deeply. I wanted it to stop. It didn't make sense to hurt this much. I'd only wanted to see her dance. That's all this was. I'd gotten attached, but that shouldn't make it hurt like this!

There was a cheery chiming from the phone, and I gaped at it breathlessly as I saw that Elaine had given me the perfect thing. It was only a voicemail, but it gave me a spark of hope. I had something of her now. I could have something to prove that this had happened. I would change my phone and number, and I would purge what remained of Elaine from my life, this small little audio clip.

Just not today.

<u>Anniversaries</u>

None of this was supposed to happen.

The thought possessed me in my entirety, staring at the series of missed calls and texts. Between Annette and Mark, I had well over twenty notifications. All of it was about wedding planning. How was there anything left to plan? Unless Annette had changed colors again. I sighed tiredly, tucking my phone in my pocket as I readied myself to leave work.

I made it as far as my car before Mark called *again.* I let the call go to the car's system, answering listlessly, "Hello, Mark."

"Seriously, dude, what the hell!"

"A good afternoon to you, too," I replied dryly, pulling out of my parking space.

Mark grumbled over the speakers, "Annette changed dates *again.* After I've already gone through the trouble of getting time out of the office! It's been three years, Li, just get it over with already."

I would never tell Mark how relieved I was that she kept finding excuses to put the wedding off. "I can't help it if she's unhappy with something, Mark."

Mark groaned loudly. "Ugh. Fine. Whatever. I guess I can find something else to do with the weekend. Hey, what about the performance arts center? Maybe there's an opera playing."

"If Annette would like to go, I don't see why not," I agreed, entirely uncaring at this point. There wasn't much else for me to do with myself anymore, not if the wedding date had been moved again.

"Right, of course, *Annette.*" I could hear Mark rolling his eyes at me. "Fine, I'll ask her."

The call ended there, making it quite clear how frustrated he was with me. I sighed quietly, focusing instead on my route home.

Today was different, I supposed. Today was Carl's and Jane's anniversary. My habits for today weren't ostentatious, nor exactly celebratory, but it was when I reminded myself that things had been different before. It had been a short time, only a few short months, and yet I needed to remember they'd happened.

I pulled into my driveway, going through the motions of returning home from work. My keys jingled on their hook; the front door clicked shut softly. Stripping off my shoes and jacket, I shambled to my study. I went to my desk immediately, rifling through the bottom drawer. I found the outdated phone easily enough, plugging it in to check the charge.

Its screen lit up instantly. My heart stopped and I pulled up the voice mails quickly. This was my one selfish indulgence, my hands trembling as I lifted the phone to my ear.

The message began to play.

"Hey, Li, it-it's Elaine. I just wanted to see if you're okay? I'm not sure what was going on earlier, but, um, anyway, I hope you're okay. Call me back soon? Bye."

The silence that followed was painful. It was always painful. Three years, and I still didn't understand why this one patient hurt me so deeply. I'd seen my sister's romance movies, but that wasn't the case with this. Elaine had always been my patient; I had always only wanted to see her well.

Right?

I tapped the screen to play the recording again, closing my eyes to listen. I could imagine her expressions still, even after so much time. I could envision her honest concern, the quiet hope that I would return her call with reassuring news. Most of all, I could see the smile she would wear when she saw me again, had I returned.

I breathed deeply, relishing in this vice. This was my one day of the year when I was wholly selfish. It was *my* day, and the only one I ever set aside to remember Elaine. Every other day, I honored my agreements and responsibilities. Every other day, those precious few months never happened.

Not today.

Cinderella Dances

Smiling to myself wistfully, I hit replay again.

~~ * ~ * ~ * ~~

"Hey. Li? Li!"

I refocused on the task at hand, realizing quickly that it was my turn. I moved my rook, announcing apathetically, "Check."

"Seriously?" muttered Mark, scowling at the pieces in frustration. He sighed as he considered his options. "So, what's got you down? Is it the wedding getting pushed back again?"

That seemed an understandably valid excuse. "It *has* gotten to be a bit of a pattern with her."

"She's got a lot on her plate." Mark shrugged. His eyes bugged wide as he cheered, making a narrow escape from my trap. "Anyway, you still get to do something this weekend. I was *just* able to get tickets to the show that's in town before it sold out."

"What's in town?" I didn't quite care, but I'd rather have company this weekend if nothing else. I detested how aggravatingly boring things became without something to break up the monotony.

"Some dance troupe. I'm not familiar, but Annette seemed pretty excited," he commented, watching me closely.

I pursed my lips, staring down at my pieces. A dance troupe? I was hoping for an opera, something visually stationary. This just hit too close to home, especially given the time of year. Maybe he hadn't realized?

"It's her, isn't it?" he guessed quickly. I sighed sharply, hoping to cut him off, but he continued, "I thought you'd be interested in it because you've been taking some lessons here and there. I didn't think she bothered you anymore, Li. She was just a patient, right?"

He knew *exactly* what he was doing.

I grit my teeth in frustration, tipping my king in forfeit with a brush of my finger. "You can see yourself out, Mark. I'll see you Saturday."

Without waiting for his reply, I left our game to lock myself in my study. I couldn't stop myself from pacing, my hands trembling as

I fought for control. This was all still too raw, that was all.

Stopping in my pacing, I stared at the drawer which held my worst of vices. Everything I had worked for—everything my family had worked for—was endangered by that one little voice mail. So why couldn't I delete it and be done with it all? She was just a patient.

But the more I stared at the drawer, the more tempted I was to enjoy that last scrap of her memory. Those were some of the happiest memories I had, sitting with Elaine in that cafe. It always felt like home; I always felt welcome.

I couldn't resist any longer, swearing under my breath at my stupidity. I found the phone quickly, and I had the message playing in an instant. Sinking into my desk chair, I sighed with a mix of relief and grief.

Elaine shouldn't have been just a patient.

The realization hit with more force than I could have anticipated, but it felt right, finally. Whatever the cost to myself, she shouldn't have been left that way. It was her life at risk, however, and that...

My denial came to an end with that final gift from Elaine. I wanted it back. I listened to my empty house, staring at my empty, tidy study, feeling like this had been nothing but a mistake. My heart ached, my eyes burned. It had to be for the better that I was finally accepting this; perhaps I could move on now.

I hit replay.

Just not today.

<u>Opening Night</u>

Tomorrow.

It was as much a thought of dread as it was a promise of anything to do that wasn't so antagonistically boring. Even my lunch break wasn't a real break anymore. It was one more reminder, a habit I'd returned to in the last few months now. Enough time had passed, I assumed it would be safe to truly go back to "before". I'd been right; the restaurant was exactly as it was before Elaine, including the extra fifteen-minute wait for a to-go order.

At least the manager didn't seem to remember me as vividly as I remembered him.

I sighed tiredly, shoving my half-eaten meal away from me, hoping my memories could go with it. What would it take to break out of this rut? I wanted to move on, but since my finally realizing Elaine's importance I felt nothing but regret. If I could just know she was okay...

I shook the thought from my mind sharply. All of that was in the past now, whether I liked it or not. It was more than time to focus on something else. I'd indulged in all of this reminiscing long enough. I was engaged, for goodness' sake!

Tomorrow, I reminded myself, finding some interest in the activities planned. *At least there's tomorrow.*

"This was a bad idea," I muttered, settling into my seat anxiously. Both Annette and Mark were acting even more strained with each other tonight. I was sat between them, trying to ignore their childish behavior.

The theater was filled with the light hum of chatter, the occasional *thump* rising out of the area of the stage. The anticipation of the show was clear all around. Tonight was exciting, and I finally perused the pamphlet in my hand for an answer. The show couldn't be that revolutionary, could it? Maybe it was the troupe performing, or their headliner—

My heart skipped, eyes going wide as I took it all in around me. It couldn't be a coincidence, could it? No. No, these seats were amazing, they had to be purchased longer than a few days ago. I took in the guilt in my companions' overly anxious features. They knew. They had to know.

I stood from my seat abruptly. "I'm leaving."

Mark was on his feet in an instant. "No, Li, you can't! The tickets—"

"You knew," I accused him, wounded too deeply to feel it all just yet. I shoved my pamphlet at him. "You knew, Mark! How *could* you?"

There was a tug on my suit jacket from my other side, bringing my attention back to Annette. I was lost for a moment as I realized that must have meant my fiancée would have known, too. I couldn't begin to guess at why she had helped Mark, but I felt like I must have failed in my duties to her along the way if she deemed it necessary.

"Li, please," she asked gently, nodding toward my vacant seat. I hesitated, obliging only in the faint hopes I better filled the role I had neglected lately. This was as much her desire as it was Mark's, it seemed. I could at least honor that.

As I settled once more, the lights of the theater dimmed to nothing, making my heart skip again. I stared at where the curtains should be, anticipation making the wait nearly unbearable. I knew I should leave. I knew I needed to just move on already, but...

It's just a show, I bargained with myself desperately.

The curtains lifted, the stage was lit, and everything I knew fell apart. I remembered someone completely different, temper modestly humbled by her reliance on others, softness aided by her naturally accepting nature. I knew someone else entirely, someone so completely wronged by circumstances.

I saw so much more of her now, gasping in awe as a young woman *danced* onto the stage. This was the woman I'd done everything in my power to help. This was the part of her I had wanted to see, that I had used to excuse so many of my actions. I could almost hear her voice in her movements, each one simply too spirited to ever have been contained by that chair. I couldn't stop myself feeling everything I had been denying and more.

This was Elaine.

Set the Stage

I thought I'd known Elaine. And, to some degree, I could admit to myself that I *had* known a part of her. Not a public side, but the calmer one that she reserved for close friends. Watching her now, I felt like I had missed so much of who she was.

There was no noticing anyone else on the stage, not for me. There wasn't a point in wasting my attention elsewhere when she seemed to command the entire show. Maybe it was poor form to stand out so much in a troupe—I didn't care. I finally saw why everyone cried the day I gave the news. I finally saw just how spirited she really was, and how completely that spirit translated into her movements.

This was what I'd wanted, for years, even without realizing it. What I'd been missing, why my home felt so empty.

By the time the curtain fell for the first intermission, I'd completely forgotten I came with anyone else. Mark's hand suddenly clapping down on my shoulder startled me from my trance. My chest tightened as I returned to reality, sitting between my best friend and my fiancée.

"That was pretty good, huh?" asked Mark in a feeble attempt at conversation. He winced as he watched me nod numbly. "Hey, are you okay? You look like you saw a ghost."

I fixed him with an incredulous glare. "I'm fine. *Great.* Why?"

"Oh, good," he laughed in relief. I'd laid my sarcasm on pretty thickly. He had to be ignoring it. "I was worried you might be mad or something."

"Or something," I offered sharply. I was still jittery from the show itself, never mind everything else that was overwhelming about tonight. "I don't think mad quite covers it."

"Oh." Mark dropped his hand from my shoulder with a nervous grin. "Right. I'll...I'll get snacks. Annette, you want anything?"

She hesitated before nodding enthusiastically. "You know what? I'll come with you."

They both shuffled toward the aisle, leaving me alone in the emptying theater. I could hear chatter from the lobby, grateful for some modicum of peace for now. I stared at the curtain, breathing deeply to help clear my head.

After a few minutes for the theater to empty a bit more, the curtains shifted. A grinning face popped through, and I recognized Elaine as she waved excitedly. Had she noticed me?! My eyes followed hers, noticing the people sitting a few rows ahead of me. They were waving back just as enthusiastically, cheering more loudly than was appropriate.

I recognized the group of friends and family a minute later. My stomach knotted with jealous regret. I should've been sitting there, too. Shouldn't I?

Elaine blew a quick kiss to her original fans before disappearing behind the curtain again. A moment later, Mark and Annette both took their seats noisily, carrying their spoils from the bar. Mark slipped a plastic cup into my uncaring grip.

"Got you your favor —Ohh-kay then," he trailed off as I threw back the double shot and shoved the cup back at him. I wasn't in the mood.

Another hour of the show in total, with one more intermission and a standing ovation. I'd never imagined that standing to applaud could cut so deeply. Even as the crowded theater patrons dispersed around us, I couldn't move. I felt locked in place, staring at Elaine's vibrant grin as she bowed and waved to her adoring audience.

I didn't want to walk away again.

That choice was made for me after another moment as Elaine curtsied her way offstage. I watched with another pang of regret, lost for a minute as I stared at the final draw of the curtains.

Mark and Annette excused themselves long before I was ready to move. It wasn't until I was certain I wouldn't see her face pop out of the curtains again that I finally left. I was the last one. Even her friends had gone, probably off to meet her for a congratulatory party. They didn't even recognize me when they passed by my otherwise empty row.

I shambled out to my car, getting in and starting the engine without thinking. My hands were frozen in place, staring at nothing as I fought to think of anything to do with myself. I couldn't go home, could I? It was so lonely there, something I'd been able to ignore until recently. I wouldn't go to Mark's. He had some explaining to do after tonight. He and Annette both.

That was it. My list of places was short, not even including my family at all. I couldn't go to them with any of this. I would get disowned if my mother didn't rip me apart first. I'd done everything I could to separate myself from this, it just wasn't enough.

Where did that leave me?

I glanced at the clock, almost surprised by the time before I finally decided on where to go. The cafe wouldn't open for another couple of hours. Still, I knew that its owners would be there—baking goods and getting ready for the day.

I couldn't care if I was speeding, but I knew I had to be to get to The Little Canary so quickly. I threw the car into park, barely remembering to take the keys with me as I rushed for the front door. My hand flew up, knocking urgently and persistently for what felt like a lifetime.

Someone gripped me from behind, spinning me around to face the short crowbar being brandished. They stopped there, confused as we recognized each other.

"Li?" Carl lowered the bar and released his grip on me. "What are you doing here? It's four in the morning."

I shuddered, finally feeling the weight of the evening prior crash into me. I shook my head slowly, biting back the flood of regret and the burn it left in my eyes.

"I made a mistake."

<u>Casting Call</u>

"That's...That's definitely the last explanation I expected," confessed Jane, sipping at her second cup of coffee. Carl had called her into the cafe early to talk so that he could continue preparing to open. I would be lying to myself if I didn't admit just how deeply I had missed this cafe and its owners.

I nodded blankly, still overwhelmed. "I'd say you could call someone to confirm, but..."

"Oh, no no, Li, no," fumbled Jane hurriedly. "Really, that's not necessary. We don't want to get you in any trouble."

"Maybe a *little* trouble..." grumbled Carl as he prepped the pastry display case.

"Carl!" she scolded in shock.

"It's not like I didn't expect some dislike, Jane, it's fine," I assured her. Carl gave a satisfied grunt at my acceptance of possible retribution on Elaine's behalf. I wasn't entirely undeserving of it. If anything, I had a fair amount of it coming.

"You didn't have the easiest choice to make, and no time to really plan it." Jane was quick to come to my defense. "I'm just glad we finally know *why*. We were all so worried, and poor Ellie—Oh! I need to call her, she needs to—"

"No!" My panic escaped me all at once, my usual professional composure at an absolute loss right now. I swallowed thickly, feeling like my heart was in my throat. It was sickening. "I don't know what to do. I just...know that I messed up."

"Well, why can't she at least know?" asked Jane hopefully, cellphone already in hand.

"I'm engaged." The words fell flat and Jane's mouth popped open in surprise. "It's an arranged marriage. I at least want to get my affairs in order, before...If-if I..."

I focused on my barely-touched cup of tea. It was long past cold by now, sipped only out of obligation for the gesture of trying to comfort me. I didn't think I could get anything in me with how knotted my stomach was.

"You've got two days," warned Carl as he leaned over the counter menacingly. Even in a flour-stained apron, he wasn't one to be taken lightly. "She's only in town another week, and I'm going to make sure she's got the time she needs for comfort."

I nodded, unsure if I feared Carl or Mother more at that moment. "That's fair."

He nodded once. "Good. And you don't come to The Canary until after, either. This is Elaine's place; it stays that way."

"Of course."

"You can call us, though," amended Jane eagerly. "Directly. I'll get you our numbers."

"Jane..." Carl sighed tiredly.

She shot him a stern look. "He's got a lot on his plate, too, Carl, what if he needs help? Or to talk?"

He frowned. "He doesn't need to talk."

"He obviously needed to talk this morning," she retorted, sounding like she'd already made up her mind on the matter. It seemed like she was just humoring his protests.

Carl rolled his eyes. "I'm going to check the muffins."

"Remember to do extra blueberries for that order," called Jane after him. She smiled and sipped her coffee. "Only call him if you can't reach me first. Okay, Li?"

I smiled and nodded, feeling more alive and welcomed than I had in years. "Okay."

~~ * ~ * ~ * ~~

Getting home was a tedious affair with how exhausted I was, but it was long overdue. With The Canary's opening, I'd left to honor Carl's declaration of it being Elaine's space. I didn't want to intrude

55

any more than I already had, and no matter how overwhelmed I was I knew I wasn't ready to face her. Not yet.

When I pulled up to my house, I groaned loudly as I recognized the car in my driveway. Why was Annette here? And so early? I glanced at the clock. Never mind.

Before I could even escape my car, she was rushing out the front door and squealing excitedly. She threw herself at me, tackling me back into my seat. I grunted in surprise, glad she hadn't knocked the wind out of me entirely.

"Li! You're not going to believe it!" she cheered excitedly, grinning widely. "Daddy's throwing a party, and he's inviting that troupe we saw last night to perform! Isn't that exciting? We get to meet them!"

"We?" I picked whatever detail I could to pretend I was engaged in her babbling enough to hide my panic.

Oh, no.

Annette giggled and tossed her hair. "Of course, silly! You're my date, *duh*."

I couldn't breathe for a long second that dragged on endlessly. Was I excited? It felt like I was excited. Just about the wrong person.

"Right. Of course," I agreed, feigning for my usually amicable, if bored, nature.

Annette didn't seem to notice anything amiss, off in her own little world. I'd never felt more grateful for her ditzy nature. "Oh, and I'm going to need you to get a costume. It's a masquerade, and you've *got* to dress up with me! I'm going to be a peacock, of course, so maybe something bird-themed?"

"I'll look into it. When's the party?" I wondered with sudden horror.

She misread it for nervousness, thankfully. "Oh, don't worry, silly, it's not until tomorrow night. You've got *plenty* of time, I'll just send my assistant over here when we're done with my costume. Okay, sugar plum?"

"Sounds good." What else was there to do but agree?

Annette giggled again, leaning forward to give me a peck on

the cheek before bouncing back to her car. She'd gotten in and driven off long before I'd found my composure enough to make it into my house. I made it as far as the entryway, shoes off and keys hung, before the crushing magnitude of the last twelve hours cascaded over me. I didn't know how to get ready for any of this. I didn't even know where to start.

I was sure of one thing—I couldn't stand how excited I was by this forced opportunity to see Elaine. Terrified and unsure, of course, and sick to my stomach with glee. This could be a second chance if I was lucky enough to figure this out. I couldn't mess this up, not again.

Please, not again.

Costumes

"I never knew I could be so anxious about picking out a *costume*," grumbled Mark as he perused his options.

Annette's assistant had been prompt in finding and arriving with costumes for the masquerade tonight. He'd even come with Mark in tow, all but dragging him by the ear. The sight of it was immensely gratifying after the stunt Mark had pulled with the show.

"Why are *you* anxious?" I managed to ask the question without any of my lingering upset reaching my voice. We could address that *after* tonight. For now, I needed to focus on my anxieties and the ridiculously stupid ideas that kept forming in my head.

My latest plot refused to leave me alone, wedged tightly in the forefront of my thoughts while I watched Mark debate his options. I knew that Elaine was going to the party, and I *had* been taking lessons. I couldn't tour the country with my dance experience, but I might keep up enough to entertain Elaine for a minute. Just a minute. Where was the harm in that? It wasn't like I'd hunted her down and broken my word. We were both going to the same event, planned by my fiancée's father.

Where was the harm?

No matter how I tried to justify it to myself, I couldn't feel the guilt I knew I should be wrestling with right now. Not for the people I should, at least. I was regretful of how everything had ended with Elaine, and I very much felt guilty over possibly opening old wounds. I could wait until after the festivities to talk, as promised to Carl.

It could wait just long enough. There was plenty of time to endure whatever more consequences my actions incurred. I just needed one dance. That was all.

Where was the harm?

"Hello? Li?" Mark snapped his fingers. "You zoned out for a minute there. Are you okay?"

"I'll be fine," I replied curtly. I nodded to his outfit to deflect his attention. "That looks good."

He took the bait easily. "Are you sure? It's not too flashy?"

"No, it's perfect. It'll even match Annette," I added offhandedly, making him flush dark red. "Don't let that stop you, Mark. You'll wear it better than her."

From there, it was just a matter of selecting my costume. Mark left by the time I'd narrowed it down to two options. As much as I wanted to be frustrated with him, Mark had been right: there was far too much anxiety in this inane activity. Why did it *matter*?!

"You have a good eye. No one would recognize you in either of those costumes," commented Annette's assistant. Had I even learned his name? The past couple of days seemed too surreal for names. "It's a pity you can't wear both!"

I gaped at my choices with a dawning sense of awe as the revelation hit me with his idle chatter.

~~ * ~ * ~ * ~~

My plan wasn't exactly revolutionary, nor was it entirely something I would be proud to claim as an actual plan.

Annette's assistant had all too happily agreed to allow me to use both costumes. He'd even agreed to my devious request to keep my selections secret. He was absolutely beside himself to think he was helping me fool his boss with a harmless little prank of switching disguises midway through the party.

While that wasn't my exact plan, it was close enough. I would find Elaine wearing my first costume, then change and pretend to be late wearing the second. I didn't know what I was intending to happen with Elaine, but...I couldn't do nothing. I knew that much.

When I arrived at the location, I felt the first wave of doubt that this was possibly a very terrible idea. The masquerade was *much* larger than I had anticipated. What I had assumed might add up to a couple of hundred people with the staff was easily double that in guests alone. It was overwhelming to think of sifting through all of those people as I passed my keys off to the valet. Climbing the steps into the impressive structure, I had to admit that my engagement to Annette was wholly advantageous to my family.

And I was putting so much at risk tonight.

That thought fell away quickly when I entered the masquerade. Everything was glittering with polish and décor, brightly lit and vibrant. The chatter of the crowds died, the sound of a violin echoing in the ensuing stillness. The next moment felt unreal as the throngs of people split to make room for the troupe preparing to perform. I had the perfect view as they lined up, my heart skipping painfully in my chest as I recognized the swan that stood front and center.

I was so close despite the distance of the floor. I thought for sure that she'd recognized me. She was staring in my direction, anyway. I couldn't care what else was happening. The music played, her troupe moved, but I didn't see anyone else. Watching her now didn't compare to the other night. I was closer here. It felt so much more tangible, even with all of the dreamlike qualities of the timing.

Elaine was right there.

Performing at my future in-laws' party.

With both of my options so plainly displayed before me, I felt foolish to know which one I'd choose. It wasn't even a choice, pushing through the crowds as the performance ended. I couldn't lose sight of that swan. I wouldn't. There was so much I needed to say, so many things to apologize for—

"Oof!"

I helped steady the swan I'd accidentally collided with, dropping my hands and staring in shock as I took in her smile.

"Oh, sorry, I don't navigate crowds well," apologized Elaine with an embarrassed shrug. She looked me over. "Hey, cool costume! Owls are neat."

<u>Performance</u>

What now?

I realized with a violent shock that I'd thought through very little of this. Should I say something? Should I not? Would she recognize my voice? Did I want her to? After all of this time, was I still not ready? And ready for what? It's not like I expected her to run away into the night with me.

Elaine was looking confused by my hesitation, and I knew I needed to do *something*.

I held my hand out to her silently, an invitation to a world I knew she couldn't resist. She stared at me for a moment longer before grinning, accepting my request by placing her dainty hand inside my gloved one, my fingers curling tight around hers. The music changed right on cue, a firm beat setting our pace as I pulled her in.

She moved with me, light and well-balanced on her feet. I remembered every video I'd seen of her, all of her favorite ways to twist with and away from her partner. That was how I'd learned to dance, imagining her as the woman I was leading in every class. So spirited and fiery, and only the strongest hand and fastest feet ever got to lead her.

I allowed her to flit away for a moment, a smirk of mischief tickling her lips. I smiled back, taking her with one hand to spin into me. She changed course, rolling across my back before I captured her in my arms again, dipping her slowly, my hand cautious of where I knew her injury had healed. She was curious now, stepping up from the dip and walking with me across the floor for several paces. I followed her lead, assenting to her control for the moment.

Like that, I knew I had her complete trust.

She turned her back to me, leaning into me, and my hand made to rest on her abdomen on instinct. Her left hand went to my face for a moment, correcting course to wrap around my neck. I sighed contentedly, loving the smell of her wafting from her hair, the smell I had missed on our walks and helping her to or from her chair.

But I knew what she wanted now, and her ankle was in my hand, her weight balanced in my arms and against my chest. I inhaled slowly, and I started to spin. This was one of my favorites of hers, and it was even more breathtaking when I was the man holding her instead of just watching.

Her fingers tapped out the seconds against my neck. Three, two, one, ready.

I let her go, dropping her with her feet only a couple inches from the floor. She hit using her momentum to twirl gracefully across the marble tiles. I hadn't realized, but the crowd had split around us as it had for her earlier, forming a large circle to give us space. Her dress looked like a storm of feathers as she forced herself to come to a stop, breathless, staring across the distance at me.

We could end it now, I thought, *just melt back into the crowd and forget each other, as we should.*

But I saw the desire on her face, the raw curiosity of what would happen if we kept on dancing. And I couldn't bear the thought of walking away now, not when we still had time left in this song and she wanted me to stay, to dance with her. This was my dream come true.

We knew. Without saying anything, we began to walk toward each other, those calculated steps that years of training burned into our muscles. I braced myself as she picked up speed, my hands catching her again. For a moment, she was held high above me, looking so much like the swan she was dressed as tonight.

Then she was falling, both of us using it to twist her around my body, slowing her descent and allowing me to catch her again mere inches from the floor. I felt it, the place where I had tried and failed to repair her, give her this chance to dance. She stared at me, her eyes burning, telling me that she heard it, too.

Our song was about to end.

I had her on her feet in another instant, hands mindful again of her injury. She spun out, pulling me with her, and we whirled across the floor again. A chorus of murmurs blended into the dying sounds of the music as we found a place where we were both comfortable, slowing ourselves. Elaine stopped, my arms still around her, and I heard her disappointed sigh. That was it. We were done.

We were both panting, winded after our whirlwind performance. I couldn't let go yet, and she wasn't stepping away, either. Everyone around us was curious, even as the atmosphere resumed as it had been before we'd so eagerly disrupted it.

"How did you know...?" she wondered softly, straining to recognize me through my mask.

It was now or never, and I wasn't in the mood to let this end yet.

"I'm just a big fan of yours, Ellie," I replied just as quietly, realizing a second too late that if my voice hadn't given me away, the nickname certainly did it.

Her face went through several expressions before she settled on shocked anger. "*You!*"

<u>Finale</u>

I can explain.

"What are *you* doing here?!"

Say it!

"I mean..." She hesitated, trying to see through my mask again. "Are you...Li?"

She sounded hopeful. Was she hopeful? I was still holding her, and she wasn't making any effort to free herself. Was that okay? Standing this close, without dancing, I felt a rush of anxious energy pounding in my chest. I performed surgeries regularly—why was I so nervous *now*?

Staring at her, it felt like I could forget the last three years apart. I didn't realize how much I'd truly missed her before. I missed our afternoons at The Canary, I missed our walks, I missed hearing her voice on the phone after I'd dropped her off at home. I'd missed Elaine.

She's waiting.

"I, erm..." I cleared my throat awkwardly, straining for a complete sentence, "Elaine—"

"Oh, my gosh, Ellie, that was fantastic!"

The shriek of joy that came next was blood-chillingly familiar, making me let go of Elaine at last. I took two paces back to be safe, startled as I watched both Annette *and* Mark hurry through the crowd. My fiancée threw her arms around Elaine with an elated giggle, while Mark...did the same.

Like old friends.

"Yeah, El, that was great!" congratulated Mark with a playful grin. "Who *was* that guy?"

I waited long enough to see that Elaine was looking for me

before melting back into the crowd. I made my way for the exit, overwhelmed by everything I was feeling now. Elaine hoped that I was me, and my best friend was acting as if they'd never lost touch. I couldn't even begin to figure out how Annette fit into all of this, but I assumed it had something to do with that ditzy attitude of hers.

And Elaine—*had* they been talking this entire time? Why did the thought hurt so much? Maybe it meant she knew already why I had to leave, or at least she had an idea? I stumbled down the first few steps before it hit me that I was leaving. This was my one chance, wasn't it? Why was I *wasting* it?

My chance for what?

I couldn't answer that. I knew what I wanted, and I knew that I'd be giving everything up, if only for a chance. There wasn't anything certain about the risk I was taking. But I *knew* that if I left now, I'd regret it. I'd go back to work, back to my terrible lunch hour, back to listening to Annette drone on and *on*. It wasn't her fault. I just knew that I wanted someone else.

Taking a deep breath, I turned on my heel to march back inside. As soon as I'd turned, I was colliding with someone again, helping steady their feathery self and stopping there.

"Elaine."

"You never answered my question," she accused me with a huff as she straightened her costume nervously. I hesitated for a moment, weighing my options.

"Well...who is this Li character, to you?" I asked, slipping my gloved hands into my pockets to keep them from shaking. After everything I'd done, did I honestly want to know the answer to that?

"That's not an easy question," she laughed. She shifted uneasily, but she was smiling, at least. "Well, at first he was just some guy I saw at lunch. Then, he was my weirdly invested doctor, who told off my really scary boss, among other things. He was my friend for a while, and then he did something I thought was selfish and I was mad at him for a while. But, um, some other friends explained things a couple of years ago, so...I guess I'm not quite so mad anymore," she admitted, blushing by the end of her explanation. Had I ever seen her blush before? I couldn't remember anymore. I wanted to rediscover it all over again, though.

I smiled, relieved to hear that she wasn't as angry as I would've expected. "I have one problem with your assessment of this guy."

Elaine blinked in surprise. "What's that?"

"I'm not weird," I contradicted her, feeling better when I heard her genuine, bubbling laugh. I sighed contentedly. "I've *missed* that sound."

"You've missed a lot," she retorted playfully, smiling broadly. She could have lit the entire street with that bright smile. She kicked one foot out in front of her. "Did you notice?"

"New shoes?" I smirked at her reaction, as she pursed her lips in frustration. I nodded. "Yes, Elaine, I noticed. I'm happy for you."

She shrugged, smiling again. "It's not entirely good as new or anything, but it's enough for me to do what I love."

"Do you need to sit and rest a moment?" I asked, realizing suddenly that we were still standing on the steps. People were walking around us, giving the occasional pointed stare.

She grinned sheepishly. "That would be great, actually. I do fine most days, but I wasn't expecting to pull off some of those moves tonight. I did *not* stretch or medicate for that."

"Perhaps...Perhaps we could continue to visit over dinner?" I suggested nervously. I was throwing caution to the wind with this, and if she said yes...

"I know this great cafe," she suggested with a nod toward the valets. "If you're interested, Doctor."

"Just Li, please," I corrected, happier than I'd been in too long. I wasn't saying goodbye yet. I wouldn't anytime soon if she was okay with that. "And if you're talking about The Little Canary, I have a request?"

"Name it," she answered eagerly, eyes glittering with excitement. Even after all of this time, she was still refreshingly spirited.

"Can you help me talk to Carl, please? He wasn't exactly a

fan of mine when I visited the other morning," I explained.

Elaine's mouth popped open for a quick second, surprised and confused, but she collected herself with a nod. "All right, Just Li, you've got a deal."

<u>Draw the Curtain</u>

I drove.

By some divine intervention, I was able to keep my eyes focused on the road. I wasn't sure if I appreciated the excuse to remain distracted, but at least I wasn't forced to pay attention to my elevated heart rate just yet. I knew I couldn't ignore the reason sitting in my passenger seat forever, though.

"So, then...you still use a chair?" I tried and failed to be casual as I referred to the equipment we had loaded into my car. Three years. *Three years* and all I could ask was *that*?

Elaine snickered at my awkward grimace. "Yeah, sometimes. I'm well enough to dance most days, but I'm never going to be like I was. I'll take what I can get."

I nodded, stopping at the upcoming light. My fingers drummed against the wheel and I glanced at Elaine in my peripheral. My eyes were back on the road just as quickly. I couldn't help feeling embarrassed that she had been watching me back. I took deep, deliberate breaths to steady my rampant pulse.

"So...what have you been up to?" she asked to break the sudden silence.

I thought back over the last three years, realizing then just how little I had *done* besides work. "Well...not much...?"

"Oh." She was quiet for a moment. "How's your cat?"

The light turned green and I had to stop myself from looking at her in surprise. "She passed last year."

"Oh, no!" she gasped, horrified. "I'm so sorry, Li. What happened?"

"I'm not sure, but she was older, so..." Despite the topic, I had to smile. No one else had ever asked about my cat. I wasn't even sure if Mark remembered my having had one.

"I'm sorry if I brought up anything painful."

"No, it's fine," I reassured her, pulling into the moderately busy lot of The Little Canary. "It's nice that you asked."

She just shrugged and smiled apologetically while I parked. I put the car in park, my hand hesitating as I reached for the keys. I turned off the car, unable to move for a minute as Elaine unbuckled herself.

"Wait." I didn't know why I stopped her from leaving. It felt like I had so much to say, but I didn't even know how to begin.

"What's wrong?" asked Elaine, peering at me through the poor lighting of the car. Did I look like something was wrong? "Li?"

Just...start.

"I..."

How? How was I supposed to put all of these thoughts and feelings into words? I'd never been the most expressive person, to begin with, and this was far from the easiest topic to address.

"Elaine, I..." I gripped the steering wheel tightly, looking at Elaine as I let out a shaky breath. "Before we go in, I...I never wanted to leave you."

"Li..."

"I didn't have a choice," I continued, for the first time hearing just how stressed it all made me. No wonder I'd gotten so many grays since then. Looking at Elaine now, I could remember that last day so vividly it hurt. "Well, I did, but...You would've lost access to your treatments. I couldn't afford to risk them, and I was blackmailed."

"Li."

"I'm sorry, Elaine." My hands were cramping from gripping the wheel so hard, but I couldn't stop. I'd been neglecting all of this for too long. I needed her to know now, while I knew I had the chance to tell her myself. She didn't seem angry, just sympathetic, and worried. "I couldn't jeopardize that for you, no matter how badly I wanted to stay."

"Da!" My first name startled me enough that I released my grip on the wheel, my hands falling into my lap. Elaine set a gentle hand on my shoulder. "I *know*, Da. Mark explained everything a few months after...But it's good to hear it from you. It makes it easier."

I stared at her for a long moment, struggling with the flood of reactions I felt. "*Mark?!*"

"And Annette," she added with a shrug, eyes bugging wide as I fell back in my seat abruptly. "Are you okay?"

I shook my head, staring out the windshield as I found some way to express this odd feeling. "They *both* knew everything? And they've been talking to you?"

Elaine nodded. "We visit when I'm in town."

I took a deep breath, this time to compose myself rather than calm my jittery nerves. I spoke as coolly as I could manage, but I couldn't curb the pain in my throat, "I missed you, Elaine. I never stopped. I-I even saved that last voicemail. I listen to it every year on the day that I...It was all I had. I didn't even have pictures. While Mark and Annette got to see you? They weren't obligated to stop, by any means, just..."

"Li?" I looked back at her, surprised to find that the topic was upsetting to her still. "I know what you mean. I was angry for a while after, too, even when they explained it all to me. None of it was fair! They wouldn't let me send anything through them. Everything was difficult. I missed you nagging and cheering me on. They wouldn't even talk about you. It wasn't fair," she said again, her words reminding me of another evening entirely. Her missed audition felt like so long ago now.

"I don't want to leave again," I told her quietly.

Elaine smiled. "I don't want you to leave again."

We were quiet for a minute while we considered what that meant. I deliberated for a moment before speaking hesitantly, "Could I get a second chance? I'm not sure what for, exactly, but I don't want to assume anything with...us."

Elaine's smile turned devious as she mulled it over a second too long for my comfort. "I think you did well the first time, all things considered. What did you have in mind?"

"I just want a chance," I realized the truth of those words as they left me. "To pick up where we left off."

"I can agree to that, *however*," she held up one hand with a solemn expression, "You need to let Annette call things off first. She's had it all planned out for ages."

"I'm...happily offended," I laughed awkwardly, but I nodded. "That sounds like a good idea, though."

"It shouldn't take her too long," she laughed with me. I'd missed that smile so much. "Until then, it's *just* coffee."

"Just coffee," I agreed, my smile fading as it hit me again that this genuinely was happening. I couldn't help myself, leaning across the center console to kiss her forehead quickly. I retreated into my seat. "I've been waiting three years for that. I just didn't know it."

"Just coffee, Li," she reminded me quietly. I couldn't tell if she was happy or sad about what I'd done. Her smile was as unrelenting as always. "Come on, I hear they've got a new flavor of muffin and it sounds *terrible*. I have to try it."

Just like that, it felt like I'd returned after leaving The Canary that day. We shared more about our time apart as we split the truly disgusting muffin she'd mentioned. Carl forgot his anger with me when Elaine couldn't stop laughing at my assessment of the garlic and onion monstrosity. He couldn't even bring himself to be upset with my critiquing.

After a while, a handful of her friends arrived, having heard through the grapevine that Elaine was visiting. No one needed explanations just yet, all of them glad to see that Elaine was happy and well. It felt like everything I'd been missing, and I knew then that I wouldn't give it up again. I was done just existing: I was ready to be happy again.

None of this was supposed to happen.

The thought possessed me, body and soul, as I took in the faces around me. Accidents happened, and life wasn't fair, but with the right company, I knew it wouldn't matter. I smiled, grateful for this chance to choose Elaine again. This time, I could stay.

This time, Elaine could dance.

<u>Encore</u>

I straightened my tie nervously, checking the time again. Not much longer until the wedding. I was just glad that Annette had finally settled on a date!

"Are the girls ready yet?" wondered Mark, his stress bleeding into his voice.

I looked him over, nodding in approval. "Perfect. I'm sure they're almost ready. Besides, it's still fifteen minutes until the wedding!"

"Do weddings *ever* start on-time, though, Li?" Mark fidgeted with his cuff-links anxiously. "How long now?"

I checked my watch. "*Still* fifteen minutes."

"What's *taking* so long?" he grumbled, beginning to pace.

"I'll go check on them," I offered, heading for the door.

Mark panicked. "No, wait! We can't see the bride before—!"

"That's *just* you, Mark, I'm only the best man," I corrected him. "So, I'm going to go check on the girls. I'll be back in a minute."

"Okay. Okay. Hey, wait, how much—"

"Fourteen minutes, Mark!"

I left our room of the church, making my way across the length of the building and through the maze of halls. I was glad that most of the guests were in the main chapel already. It saved me having to dodge people along the way to the decorated door of the bride's dressing room.

I knocked once, grinning when Elaine opened the door. Her iridescent aquamarine gown looked like it would have been over the top on anyone else, but her dancer's grace lent her the confidence the outfit needed.

"You're not supposed to see the bride before the wedding," she teased with a smirk.

"Are you asking me something?" I replied, winking playfully. I loved that I could still make her blush. "Anyway, I'm here to check on you ladies, on behalf of a very excited Mark."

"He's panicking, isn't he?" she guessed in a whisper.

"Oh, yeah, he's panicking." I nodded, laughing at it all. I still couldn't believe that *Mark* was marrying Annette. It turned out that they'd gotten to know each other over the years of helping Elaine come to terms with my absence. I couldn't be upset about any of it these days. Annette had offered me a remarkable opportunity working at her father's medical clinics, along with company shares to apologize for the retracted marriage plans.

Not that I'd expected such generosity. I had been ready to lose everything if it meant a chance to have more than "just coffee" with Elaine.

"I'm ready!" cheered Annette gleefully from somewhere deeper in the room.

"That's my cue to go calm the groom down and drag him to the altar," I hummed, making Elaine giggle. She shifted her stance with a visible wince. "I'll have your chair ready on the sidelines for you, Ellie. Between the wedding and your recent tour, you haven't had time to rest properly."

She smiled, ducking out of the room enough to give me a peck on the cheek. "Thank you, Da. You know how to treat a girl."

"I know how to treat *you*," I contradicted, turning on my heel to fetch Mark. "I'll send a text when we're heading to the chapel!"

"'Kay!"

Checking my watch again, I gaped at the time before sprinting down the halls. *Now* we were running late! As long as Mark hadn't had a total breakdown, we could still be fashionable about everything. I breathed a sigh of relief as I approached. He was already waiting in the hall.

"You ready?" I panted, stopping to catch my breath.

Mark nodded jerkily. "I-I think so."

"Good. We need to go. Oh!" As we started back toward the chapel, I texted to let the girls know we were on our way with one hand, fishing a chess piece from my pocket with the other. I handed Mark the king with a smile. "For good luck, and as your wedding present."

He laughed at the gesture, pocketing the king with a grin. "I knew I'd get it someday."

"Enjoy it for now," I told him, steering us toward the chapel doors. We came out just behind the altar, taking our places quickly. I couldn't resist the impulse to scan the crowd, disappointed more than I should have been.

"It's all right, Li, your family will come around eventually," whispered Mark when he saw my smile break slightly. "And even if they don't, you've always got us and The Canary."

"You're right," I agreed quietly. Our hushed conversation was interrupted by the organ roaring to life to announce the bride's approach. While everyone else was watching for Annette, I couldn't take my eyes off of Elaine. The bridesmaids all walked alone, as per Annette's demands. We still hadn't heard the end of how awkward it would look for only one of her party to be walked by me, and Mark didn't have anyone else he wanted to stand by him.

It was still beautiful, and Mark still cried. Annette cried. The guests cried. I only held out until I finally glanced at Elaine in her gorgeous gown, thinking of one day, when she was ready for more than "just coffee"...I cried, too.

Everything rushed by, and before I knew it we'd made it to the reception. Mark and Annette's first dance was beautiful, but I was busy helping Elaine settle into her chair. She truly had been overextending herself lately, and every time I'd seen her this last month she'd been in some sort of discomfort.

Leaning down, I spoke quietly beside her ear, "Is there anything I can get you, Ellie?"

"Mm, I don't think so. It's been a while since you came included with a morphine drip," she replied with a playful smile. She looked up at me. "I'm okay, really. I'm taking the next couple weeks off, for personal reasons."

"Maybe you can help me move my girlfriend in with me?" I offered jokingly.

"Maybe. I've got time."

I stopped short in surprise. "That's a bit more than coffee, Ellie."

She grinned at my reaction. "I think I'm ready for more than coffee, Da."

I couldn't stop my giddy laugh. The first dance was ending, other guests meandering onto the dance floor now. "May I have this dance to celebrate?"

Elaine looked down with a sad sigh. "Li..."

Setting my hands on her shoulders, I swayed in place behind her. Realizing what I was doing, her face lit up. She placed her hands atop mine, swaying her head in time with me.

"You really don't mind?" she asked self-consciously.

"Not at all, Elaine," I reassured her happily. My family may have still been denying me, but Mark was right—I had The Canary, Elaine's extended family. As much as I missed my family's weekly dinners, I hadn't felt alone in the slightest lately. It was such a relief. Leaning down again, I murmured, "This might be a bit forward, Ellie, but I think this is a good venue to tell you...I *really* like you."

"Oh, that's very forward," she laughed. "But I like you, too. *Like* like."

I gave her a peck on the cheek in reply, enjoying it all today. It was perfect. It wasn't even my wedding, and I thought it was perfect. I couldn't be anything but happy when I danced with Elaine.

More titles by Karma Rose:

Demon Rising
Broken Orbit

Coming 2021:

Satellites and Shooting Stars
Angel Falling

Meet Cory Charles Lawrence:

Farmer, family man, and...demon?

Painting the life of a demon raised human, *Demon Rising* follows Cory Charles Lawrence, from his youth to modern day. In a world where demons have recently gained rights, the dangers Cory faced as a child are far from over. With the aid of Robert, his therapist, Cory seeks to make sense of a world he barely recognizes and a life he cannot remember.

<u>Prologue</u>

Robert Smith possessed a more than generic name, had lived an average life as a therapist—working with average patients—and adored his wife and two children. He had come to discover that the level of life he had achieved was unsatisfying and unbearably dull. He went to work six days a week to pay for his suburban home and ensure his children a place in decent colleges.

The repetitive schedule had begun to drill a numbing hole in his skull where he could feel all of his life's potential leaking from.

When the elite researchers, studying a sentient, as-of-yet-unnamed specie tapped his shoulder then, he was thrilled to accept the job. They wanted him to evaluate their specimen to see if it was stable enough to be released into society. A wonderful change in pace to Mr. Smith; a break away from the ordinary. How hard could it have been to speak to it? After all, even the press called it an animal.

Arriving at the institute—trimmed brown hair combed back neatly and brown eyes sparkling with anticipation—he was unnerved by the number of halls they took him down. First one, then to the left, then the right and back again. It was enough to drive him mad before, at last, his guide stopped at a plain silver door. Robert smiled tentatively.

"Is this it?" he asked, nervous now that he was genuinely there.

The guide nodded, "Yeah. He's in there. And don't worry, he's not half as terrifying as he looks."

Robert's eyes widened as the guide walked away. He stared at the door a moment longer before taking a deep breath to steady himself. He turned the knob and the door swung open noiselessly.

He was surprised to find the creature look up at him with a start when he entered the room. To be honest, Robert was shocked to see it. It was tall, to be sure, even when sitting and appeared as though it could have modeled for David were it not for the rich crimson skin. It had large, leathery wings and a snaking tail that ended in a broad arrow-head the size of Robert's hand. Two thick horns, of varying shades of brown, grew from its forehead and curved over its skull to the back of its head.

The beast watched Mr. Smith with bright green eyes set beneath heavy brows. "Good morning, sir. I would have dressed more appropriately had I known you were going to look so sharp."

Robert glanced down at his navy blue suit, frowning in confusion. "Ah, right. Erm, am I understanding correctly that you're the…patient?"

The demon chuckled and Robert's stunned mind was able to notice how deep the demon's voice was, causing him to shudder. "Such a polite term compared to what I have become accustomed to, but yes. Please, sit. I was told the appointment could last all day and no man I have met has stood that long before."

Robert nodded. Straightening his jacket nervously, he sat across from the demon with a sigh, setting his bag by his feet. His eyes widened when he realized that his suit matched the color of the demon's lips perfectly. "Are you alright?"

The demon nodded politely, "Yes, sir. Why do you ask?"

"Your lips! They're blue," cried Robert, outraged. It spoke like a person! How could these researchers mistreat it so horribly? Was there something they had not told him? He refrained from glancing at the door in his mild trepidation.

"Of course, sir, that is their natural color," replied the demon calmly, touching a curved claw to his pointed chin, appearing thoughtful, "Although, I do appreciate your concern."

Robert cleared his throat, sighing again. This was the strangest day he could recall ever having, "Right. So, let's get this started." He pulled a pen and pad of paper from his bag. "What's your name?"

"Cory Charles Lawrence," answered Cory, fidgeting and glancing at the door.

Robert frowned. "Is something wrong?"

"I apologize. I have nervous issues regarding an unending list of things that I am certain we will address at one point or another," sighed Cory, closing his eyes. Robert waited patiently for the demon to recover. Eyes snapping open, Cory waved a hand to Robert. "Please, continue."

"How old are you?"

"I will be 68 on the ninth of August."

Robert glanced at the demon's youthful appearance incredulously. "And how long have you been at this facility?"

"Forty-one years, tomorrow," murmured Cory, eyes becoming distant. He sighed heavily, leaning back in his chair. He stared at his hands tearfully, "A very long time, sir. One's appearance, in every sense, can change drastically, their life even more so. You look like a young man. How old are you?"

Robert blinked in surprise. He had never had a patient ask him that before. "Forty-six."

"Mm, young indeed. Do you love your wife?" he asked, pointing to Robert's ring.

"Immensely," replied Robert reflexively.

Cory nodded. "Do you have any children?"

"Two girls. Why are you asking all of this?" inquired Robert, pen poised. Whatever the reason, it was sure to be useful in his diagnosis.

Cory smiled with a doleful look in his eyes, revealing a few sharply pointed teeth. "Forty years alone is…brutal. I find it comforting to know that others can still enjoy what I lost. When did you propose?"

"When I was twenty-four. Why do you find it comforting?"

A glistening droplet streaked down the demon's angular face. "It helps me imagine my life, had I not been brought here. From what I recall I was twenty-seven, bound to inherit a farm outside of a small town I called home. It was the most I could ever ask for being what I am and it was the curiosity of this facility that…Well, I would be impolite to finish that sentence, so I will not. Do you understand why it is I ask to know if a wife, children and home are enjoyable?"

Robert nodded numbly, pale skin paling further as an alien guilt shivered up his spine. "Yes. Yes, I do. Can you tell me what it was like for you growing up?"

Cory's eyes slid half-shut and became distant, but he nodded. "Yes. I remember all of it quite well and I miss it. Would you like me to make it a story for you, sir, since you seem so intrigued?"

"Please, do. I'll stop you if I have any questions that can't wait."

"Well, then. Let me see how best to begin…"

About the Author

Karma Rose was an unschooled student and has always been a writer at heart. Although she began with poems and short stories, she has now since completed two installments in her *Gravity* series, *Demon Rising* and its sequel, *Broken Orbit*. She spends her days tending her small farm.

For updates on current and future projects, look for Karma Rose on various social media platforms!